KT-104-579

The Tall Stranger

With the Sioux defeated, land along the Powder River was up for grabs. Some violent men were after it but they hadn't bargained for hunter and guide Lonesome Brad Bradshaw.

When rancher Rob Henshal was shot from the saddle, Brad rode into rumbustious Miles City intent on bringing the backshooter to justice. Could it be shyster lawyer Charles Horniblow? Or psychopath Scarface Jack Mosby? Were the Diamond Square cowboys on the level? Or was Rob's neighbour, the fiery Euala del Toro, behind the rustling?

The arrival of pretty easterner Heather Monro adds further fuel to the fire as she, too, lays her claim to the ranch. Against all the odds can Brad rescue Heather from peril and nail the killer?

By the same author

Black Pete – Outlaw
The Last of the Quantrill Riders
Duel at Silverillo
Death at Sombrero Rock
The Train Robbers
The Lawless Land
The Gambling Man
The Maverick
The Prairie Rat
Bullwhip
The Crooked Sheriff
The Montana Badmen
Lousy Reb
The Black Marshal
Blood Brothers
The Hanging of Cattle Kate
Bad Day at San Juan
Bushwhacked!
A Town Called Troublesome
Sidewinder
Horse Dreamer
The Horsehead Trail
Rogue Railroad
Canyon of Tears
Rattler
They Came to Riba
The Black Sheriff
Journey of Death
Two Shots for the Sheriff
Death at the Corral
The Lost Mine
Stolen Horses
River of Revenge

The Tall Stranger

JOHN DYSON

A Black Horse Western

ROBERT HALE · LONDON

© John Dyson 2005
First published in Great Britain 2005

ISBN 0 7090 7749 1

Robert Hale Limited
Clerkenwell House
Clerkenwell Green
London EC1R 0HT

The right of John Dyson to be identified as
author of this work has been asserted by him
in accordance with the Copyright, Designs and
Patents Act 1988.

Typeset by
Derek Doyle & Associates, Shaw Heath.
Printed and bound in Great Britain by
Antony Rowe Limited, Wiltshire

ONE

Lonesome Brad Bradshaw made his camp beneath a blueberry thicket in a cherry-grove along a creek of the Cannonball River. He had covered fifty miles that day and planned to make himself comfortable before night set in. It might be early May but there was little sign of summer. The creek was still edged with ice and it got brittle cold at night. For some reason he felt uneasy as he hauled a young buck, roped by its antlers, to hang from a branch, and skilfully used his razor-sharp Bowie to slit the hide from belly to throat. There would be enough meat to more than last him the rest of his 400 mile journey.

'What's that?' A shrill, croaking bird's cry had broken the gloomy silence of the woods. He paused, knife in hand, and looked over his shoulder, peering through the branches all around him. Maybe it was a bird. An oriole, or some such migrant. 'I'm gittin' jittery, ' he muttered to the horse who was loose-hitched, grazing nearby.

He stoked up his stone fireplace with sweet-scented cedar- and cherry-logs he had axed, and set to skinning and butchering the buck.

'I gotta stop talkin' to the hoss,' he said. 'It's a crazy habit.But a man's gotta talk to somebody.'

Brad was a tall man, broad-chested, with a mop of tousled black hair. He was in his late twenties, weathered like oak, with already a map of lines around his slits of eyes as if he had spent too many years squinting through harsh sunlight or snow blizzards.

With the ease which came of experience he hacked himself a thick steak which he skewered with a prong of greenwood. He placed it across two forked sticks to broil over the blaze. He had already made himself a bed of pine needles to protect him from the ground's damp and cold, and erected a shelter of boughs above it. He poured himself a mugful of coffee from his pot and sat down to rest his weary body against the big Denver saddle.

Not having anything else to read, he pulled the letter from his shirt pocket and studied it once again. He had found it awaiting him at the railroad depot and by then it was already a month old. It was written in scratchy ink on blue paper.

Dear Brad,

I hope this finds you. This may come as a surprise but I'd like to offer you the post of ranch foreman here at $100 a month all found. The stock's prospering. I got eight other boys on the payroll. I been having problems

6

*with thieving rustlers. It ain't nothing you and I can't
handle. I know you never much cared for prodding
cows, but it's time you settled down. I been thinking,
maybe I could cut you in as equal partner. If you agree
come as fast as you can.*

It was signed *Rob* and bore the address of the
Diamond Square ranch on the Powder River,
Montana.

Brad took a sip of the coffee and pursed his lips,
considering. There was a note of urgency to the
missive, almost of desperation. Rob Henshall hadn't
had a lot of luck lately. His wife, Alice, had died in
childbirth, the baby with her. When he got the letter,
Brad felt that it was up to him to help out. Anyway, he
wasn't doing anything. But why would Rob make
such a generous offer?

For the past winter Lonesome had been working
as hunter and guide for the North Pacific Railroad
company out of Bismarck, which was just a collection
of shacks in those days on the far side of the Missouri,
and terminus of the line from Chicago. But the
company had long had grandiose plans for extend-
ing the track across North Dakota as far as Miles City
and on up through to northern Montana. Brad's job
had been to provide game to feed the tracklaying
crew and lead the surveyors in a line as straight as the
crow flies some 400 miles to the 'city' on the
Yellowstone. It had been a tough operation and had
been only half-way done when funds fizzled out.

None of the workers had been paid for a month or more and the shipments of iron rails and ties had failed to arrive. When Bradshaw returned to base he found the company was having financial problems due to the recent crash of the banks, and Rob's letter waiting for him. So he saddled his bronc and headed west north of the Standing Rock reservation and along the Cannonball figuring it would be the easiest route to reach the Powder River.

Since the Custer massacre in 1876, four years earlier, the army had moved in to subdue the Sioux and Cheyenne by heavy force of arms. Most of them were safely on the various reservations and white men had not been slow to step in to carve up the rich grazing lands of the plains bordering the Yellowstone. Robert Henshall had been one of the first to seize the opportunity and within a couple of years had built up a good herd. Everything had looked hunky-dory.

Bradshaw tucked the letter back in the pocket of his blue wool shirt. Like Rob said, he had never until then been much interested in cows. Nor, for that matter, in slaughtering buffaloes. He was a self-educated man with a fondness for books and a preference for his own company and lone exploration of the wilderness, which had earned him his soubriquet.

While out on the trail he liked to keep himself as neat and tidy as he could, even to washing his clothes and having a shave and a bath every month. That alone put him apart from most of the smelly, hairy, louse-ridden varmints who roamed the plains. Brad wouldn't dignify them with the word hunters. What skill was there in slaughtering a hundred beasts at a stand with their powerful long-range rifles, taking the robes and leaving the bloody carcasses to rot?

Not that Brad didn't have his own long-range rifle, a Winchester '76, which he had propped over against a rock. As well as his solid Remington six-gun, he generally carried a Spencer seven-shot slung across his back. A hunter had to be ready for anything. He quickly reached for this and rose to one knee as the bird's shrill cry echoed through the woods, closer now, to receive an answering call. The hair on his nape bristled as he jumped up to one knee and levered a slug into the breech. He had a strong sense he was being watched. Could it be Sioux?

There were still hostile renegade bands roaming about. A few of Sitting Bull's warriors had been raiding down from Canada. And Rain-In-The-Face, the Hunkpapa, had vowed never to give in. Bradshaw prowled forward away from his camp-fire. He had built it in the dense thicket, hoping that its smoke would disperse. But maybe they had been following him.

He stepped silently, careful not to step on dry branches or give himself away, making a slow circuit of his camp, getting down on his belly to crawl in places through the tangle of blueberries. Waiting, listening, searching . . . but there was no sign or sound.

'Hot damn,' he hissed to himself as he returned to the fire. 'A man can't be on guard every minute of the day.' That was the one problem with being a loner. A man was kinda vulnerable. He laid the Spencer aside carefully, some distance from the fire. 'Aw, hell,' he growled. 'My steak's burning.'

He was as hungry as the proverbial hunter. With his fingers he fished from the glowing ashes a hunk of sourdough, nicely baked, which he placed on his wooden platter along with the steak. This was beautifully brown and 'crumpy' outside and red and juicy within. He gave it a dusting of cinnamon sweetening. He pulled on his navy-blue ex-army topcoat, lined with Missouri blanket, for his back was chilly, even if his knees were scorching, as he hunkered down on his saddle to enjoy the repast.

'Food for the gods,' he whispered. 'What more could a man want than some good ol' plum duff and custard? But I guess we'll have to wait for that.'

Lonesome Bradshaw figured he could cook as well as any woman so what need had he for a squaw? Well, apart from the obvious. He was a healthy man in his prime and had to admit he often hankered for the company of a woman. He was not one of those who cared to pay for the favours of the depraved harpies of the stockade saloons. So there he had another problem. He had been involved for three years with one woman, without benefit of clergy. Denise was her name. Even now it sounded like a sneer. That two-timing twister who had hypnotized and fascinated him. He gave a snort of indignation.

'Never again. There's nothing worse than a crooked woman.'

He sighed, his belly full, and tossed the empty platter aside, starting to fill his pipe. It would soon be dark. He would be on his way before first light. It was then that he met their eyes, looking up and seeing them suddenly there: three painted warriors stepping silently out of the scrub on moccasined feet, weapons raised threateningly. They had him at their mercy.

They stood in a triangle about him, their dark faces savage, their eyes merciless. One, in a buffalo-horn mask, held a feathered lance clutched in his fist, its honed-flint point aimed at his chest. A second, in leggings, breechclout, a faded cavalry jacket and forage cap – which indicated he had already been on the rampage – held a bow, its string pulled taut, the arrow ready to pierce his throat. And the third, near-naked but for a long, flowing loin-cloth, a porcupine-quill breastplate and, oddly, a big crucifix hanging from his neck, held aloft a scalp-hung tomahawk.

Brad's first inclination was to kick the coffee-pot and burning logs at them and go for his Remington sidearm, but he knew that before he could get it from the greased scabbard, fast as he was, the arrow would thud into him, the lance would disembowel him and soon his own hair would be dangling from the tomahawk. In other words, it would be suicide.

So, instead, he slowly rose, raising his hands, fingers outstretched, and said in his quiet manner: 'Howdy, fellas, you wanna sit down and have some coffee and a puff of my pipe?'

He repeated the question in Siouan, saying they were welcome to his camp and a bite to eat. 'The war's over, boys. I ain't got no argument with you folk.'

That didn't appear to cut much ice with these natives. They stood, their weapons poised, waiting for the slightest false move. Bradshaw noticed from the beadwork of the moccasins they must be Minneconjou and tried again.

'Whose tribe are you with? Red Panther's? I know him. We've smoked together. He and I are old friends.'

The one with the lance prodded him, its sharp point pricking into his chest.

'No white man friend. All white men spies, enemies. Why we not kill you?'

Brad shrugged and tried to look unworried, although he could feel his heart pounding alarmingly. It wouldn't do to show them he was scared. The Sioux gave great credit to courage.

'Why should you kill me? I ain't harming you.'

'All white men spies,' the tomahawk one repeated more vehemently, moving in to draw Brad's revolver carefully from its scabbard. He clutched it with satisfaction, dropped the tomahawk and fired off a shot at a tree-bole. The noise sounded startlingly loud in

Item(s) Borrowed

Branch: Tillydrone Library
Date: 10/09/2021 **Time:** 10:33 AM
ID: 63356000718387

ITEM(S)	DUE DATE
The tall stranger............................ X0000000347850	08 Oct 2021

Your current loan(s): 2
Your current reservation(s): 0
Your current active request(s): 0

Please retain this receipt and return items on or before the due date.

Thank you for using Aberdeen City Libraries.

https://www.aberdeencity.gov.uk/services/libraries-and-archives

Tel 03000 200293 or 01224 652500

the woods' silence. The Indian grinned and fired two more shots. As acrid powder-smoke curled he turned the long-barrelled six-gun on the white man. 'You got whiskey?'

'Nope. I don't carry it. I know you guys can smell it from twenty miles away. Anything else you want I'm willing to trade.'

At that, the one in the army cap and coat gave a scoffing laugh.

'We do not trade. We take.' He lowered his bow, keeping the arrow fixed but releasing the tension from the string, and sprang across the fire to pick up the heavy rifle and brandish it skywards. 'This mine.' He gave a whoop. 'You got bullets?'

'That's a hundred-dollar gun, friend.' Bradshaw was beginning to get mad instead of scared. 'I would-n't advise you to take that.'

'We take everything.' The one in the buffalo horns prodded him with the lance again. 'Everything. Your coat, your shirt. Take off.' He made an impatient movement with the lance. 'Now!'

The other warriors began to laugh among them-selves. A white man without his guns was just a tooth-less dog. They began to poke about among his kit as the lance-man ordered Brad to strip. It dawned on him what they were planning. *The Race for Life.* He would be given a chance to make a run for it. Naked. Rare for it not to end in death.

What could he do but obey or die?

'This ain't right, boys,' he protested, down now to

13

his flannel, faded-red long johns. 'At least let me keep my boots.'

The masked one tore the flannel with his lance tip and Brad resignedly removed his last vestments, even his thick woollen socks. The other two gave shrieks of victory and began loading all his belongings on his horse, his meat, his clothes, his rifle, cinching the saddle and fixing them fast. Brad was beginning to feel more than lonesome.

No man cares to stand stark naked in front of grinning, jeering enemies, and he winced as the lance-man prodded him on his way.

'You go,' the Sioux shouted in his own language. 'We chase. We kill you.'

'This sure is unfriendly, boys, but if that's the way you want it.' Brad began hopping away, a bramble piercing his bare toes, his buttocks white and gleaming in the dying rays of the sun which filtered through the tree-branches. The Indians laughed loudly. They seemed to find his plight hilarious.

Brad went skipping down the creek for fifty paces, tripped and 'fell', groping for the Spencer he had hidden beneath a boulder. He turned on one knee, levering it with practised expertise.

'Laugh, would you?' he called, as their faces froze. He took out the one with the Remington. The revolver exploded, the bullet going wild as the Indian was bowled over. 'Maybe that'll wipe the smile from your faces,' Bradshaw whispered.

The two remaining Sioux stood poised like a frieze,

until the one with the lance gave a scream of rage and hurled it at him. Bradshaw rolled aside as it hissed past to thud into a tree, and came up, relevering the carbine. He put a bullet between the thrower's eyes.

The third Sioux tried to pull his arrow. Bradshaw, cold and determined, fed another slug into the seven-shot. Again he made no mistake. The cavalry-uniform-clad Indian gave a retch of agony as the lead ploughed into his chest.

'You shoulda killed me, boys,' the white man said, as he stood with the smoking carbine, 'instead of just talkin' about it.'

They all were still, laid in the contractions of death. Naked, Brad turned and looked around him in case there were others lurking in the woods. He went to grab at the piebald's mane, soothing the startled prancing horse.

'OK, gal.'

Suddenly, another shot barked out and the mare went plunging down, blood gouting from her throat. Bradshaw stepped back from the kicking hoofs, turned and saw the slender, near-naked Indian, raised on one elbow, the revolver in his hands, aiming another shot. Brad pumped a bullet into him. He screamed and fell back.

Brad walked gingerly across and put his last three bullets into their heads ar close quarters.

'Ain't it funny how you damn Indians come back to life,' he growled, picking up his Remington and returning it to his holster. 'I shoulda made sure of you.'

He returned to the mare, but she was kicking her last, blood pumping out.

'Sorry, ol' gal,' he said, drawing the revolver and putting a bullet through her temple. 'You were a good pal.'

He dressed himself hurriedly, worried that there might be others of the war party in the vicinity. 'That was a fifty-dollar horse,' he muttered, angrily. 'Those thieving varmints. All the damn trouble they cause. Still, I guess you cain't blame 'em. They ain't had the best of deals.'

He scouted around with the reloaded Spencer, hoping to find their ponies in the woods, but there was no sign or sound of them. Not a snicker. It was getting too dark to look for hoof-prints. He came to the conclusion they must have been left in the care of a young boy, who, after witnessing the mayhem, had high-tailed it as fast as he could back to his camp.

'Aw, hell,' Brad muttered. 'Don't look like I'm gonna get any shut-eye tonight.'

He decided it would be best, before any others came looking for vengeance, to travel by night and head back to the Missouri fifty miles on foot. The saddle would be a heavy load to carry but he ought to be able to make it in two nights' walking. 'I ain't leaving the rifle or the carbine,' he growled, as he tied them to it, and hefted it all over his shoulder. He started off back along the creek to the Cannonball.

Soon the moon would rise and guide him on his way.

'Thunderation! A fine kettle of fish this is. Still, I guess I'm lucky to still have my hair.'

TWO

'We're well in the lead.' Lieutenant Claud Page was ecstatic as he stood on the bridge of *The Far West*. 'Fifty dollars for you, Captain, if we're first into Miles City,' he shouted.

'Damn fool,' Grant Marsh muttered under his breath, and added loudly: 'We need to call in at Poverty Point for more wood. If I put on any more steam the boilers will start spitting rivets.'

Captain Marsh swung the wheel on the open bridgehouse of the shallow-draught steamer as its rear paddle thrashed, churning them on their way, fighting the powerful current. It was the May rise when the wide Missouri River was at its highest and in full flow, fed by the melting snows of the Rockies.

The crusty old riverboat pilot kept a wary eye alert for any snags or dangers as he swung the vessel in towards the west bank, but his broad chest, too, swelled with pride to know that he had left the *Star of the Plains* well in their wake.

Behind the bridgehouse, which was perched for'ard above a double row of salon, kitchens and small cabins, a young lady, Heather Monro, was seeking shelter from the stiff wind, but she, too, was caught up in the excitement of the race as she saw the drifting smoke from the tall stacks of the rival steamboat on the horizon several miles behind them.

Heather was wrapped in an ankle-length purple velvet topcoat, woollen muffler and matching purple hat pulled low over her brow. Summer was slow to arrive in these northern parts. *The Far West*, she noticed, was swinging across towards a small cabin built on a promontory of the river bank, and a makeshift log jetty jutting out into the water.

So far there hadn't been much of interest to be seen on the banks of the mighty Missouri River: mostly flat, empty plains disappearing into the mists, or a glimpse of some despondent-looking Indians, wrapped in blankets on stunted ponies, watching as if from another world. She could see cord-wood piled high by the jetty so guessed this was a fuel-loading station. What a lost and lonesome place for anyone to spend their days.

A shabby man in a coonskin cap waved to welcome their approach as Captain Marsh eased *The Far West* in alongside the jetty, putting the paddles into half-astern. The man ran to catch a rope that was tossed to him and secured it fast.

There was only one other, younger, man to be seen, his six-foot height made taller by his high-heeled boots and Stetson hat. His broad shoulders were encased by a navy-blue topcoat and he wore a blue-speckled bandanna loose around his throat. There was an intriguing air of mystery about him. What was he doing, Heather wondered, out in these parts on his own so far from civilization?

Before the wood-cutter began loading his logs, the stranger hefted a saddle rig over one shoulder and stepped along the wobbly jetty to the even more precarious gangplank.

'Got a cabin to Miles City?' he called up to the captain before stepping aboard, then his eyes met those of the girl. His somewhat sour countenance became more alert as he tipped a finger to his hatbrim in acknowledgement of her, and his lips flickered to one side in what Heather could only describe as a somewhat cynical, or mocking grin. His jowls were covered in four weeks' growth of black stubble and the walnut butt of a big revolver jutted from a holster slung on one hip. She was not sure she liked the look of him, so she turned and strolled aft. At least a gleam of sunshine was penetrating the Montana murk. Perhaps summer was on its way at last.

'Heather, you can't possibly wear that dress,' her Aunt Maud snapped. 'It makes you look like a saloon tart.'

'Why, what's wrong with it?' the girl protested. 'It's the latest fashion in Boston.'

'Boston! This isn't Boston. That bustle thing. And the neckline, it's positively indecent. Not that you've got much to show.'

Heather smoothed the tight sleeves of the green velvet dress and hitched her decolletage a little higher. Admittedly, the waist was wasp-tight. She wished she'd stayed in her day-frock now. 'It was you who told me to dress in my best for dinner, Aunt, and this is all I've got.'

How tired she was of being cooped up with this disapproving old termagant, first on the railroad to Omaha, then in the hotel rooms, and now this cabin. For her Aunt Maud nothing was ever right with the world.

'Indeed? We want to make an impression on Lieutenant Page, but, really, what will he think?' Her aunt had already strongly intimated that Lieutenant Claud Page, just out on the frontier from West Point, would make a very 'handsome catch'. His family, she had discovered, was old New England and not unwealthy.

'Well, I'm not changing now.' Heather wrapped a loose chiffon scarf around her throat and arranged it to cover her offending bare chest. 'Perhaps that will shield me from male gaze, do you think? Do I pass?'

'There's no need to be impertinent, Heather. Young people should show a little respect for their elders. Come, that was the dinner-gong. Try not to eat too eagerly and take your cue in the conversation from me.'

21

'But I'm starving and I like talking to the captain. He's very interesting. Did you know he navigated all the way up the Yellowstone and took injured off after the Little Big Horn disaster?'

'He is not of our class.'

What a wag Lieutenant Page was! In his spanking new uniform, with its gleaming gilt buttons and epaulettes, he would spend the evenings pounding away at the ancient upright pianoforte in *The Far West*'s saloon, singing in a somewhat cracked tenor a wide selection of popular airs. Always up to something. The life and soul of the party.

'How dull this trip would have been without you along,' Aunt Maud flattered him over dinner. She nudged Heather with her elbow indicating she should join in the adulation, but Heather was busy dealing with a rather bony trout. 'How long a tour of duty are you on, might I ask? Are many of the officers at Fort Keogh married?'

'Oh, yes, quite a good few.' Page glanced over-eagerly at Heather. It was plain he was smitten by her modest charm, her softly curled light-brown hair encompassing her delicate, intelligent features. Her heather-grey eyes in wide whites gave her, he thought, the air of a startled fawn. 'The officers' family quarters are very spacious, well away from the enlisted men's barracks and the stables. He smiled at the girl. 'I would recommend them.'

Heather frowned and dipped her fingers in the

water-bowl then wiped them on her napkin.

'The other passenger?' she asked Captain Marsh. 'Isn't it rude not to invite him to join us at dinner?'

'Heather, don't be absurd,' her aunt interrupted. 'He's not one of us. A dangerous look about him. Didn't you see the two rifles he was carrying and the revolver. I wouldn't be surprised if he's some lawbreaker, a wanted character.'

'How can you say that?' Heather protested. 'You know nothing about him.'

'Neither do I,' Captain Marsh, at the head of the table, drawled. 'Never seen the guy before. Just some wandering saddle bum is my guess. He said his hoss had got killed. That's why he's travelling with us. I had him served dinner in his cabin. Guess he's happy enough.'

'Oh, come on, Captain.' Lieutenant Page affected to take Heather's side. 'This is the United States, a true democracy, especially out here in the West. We don't pull rank. Invite him up for a drink.'

Heather thought that the lieutenant had probably already had enough, himself, which was what was making him so effusive. She jumped as Page, who was seated alongside her, patted her knee.

'That was very nice,' she said, to cover her confusion. 'Did you say buffalo-steak was next course, Captain?'

'That's right,' Marsh replied, as his cook's galley hand cleared their plates. 'Or elk. Whatever you fancy. You sure got a big appetite, young lady.'

'It must be all this fresh air.' Heather smiled, quickly rearranging her chiffon scarf, for the lieutenant was leaning forward apparently fascinated by her decolletage.

When coffee and brandy were being served Captain Marsh went to invite the stranger to the saloon.

'He's a surly-looking sonuvagun. I hope he knows how to behave himself.'

Brad sauntered into the steamer's saloon sometime later with the rolling gait of a man who spent much time in the saddle.

'Howdy, folks,' he drawled, with his thin-lipped, caustic grin. 'Nice of you to invite me to join your li'l party.'

Heather couldn't be sure that he wasn't being sarcastic. He had discarded his Stetson, spurs, gunbelt and topcoat, appeared to have tugged a comb through his unruly black hair, but he still had a heavy stubble.

'Come and join us,' she said, indicating one of the battered armchairs arranged around the pot-belly stove.

'If you don't mind I'll seat myself upwind,' Aunt Maud remarked, giving a sniff of her haughty nostrils in his direction. 'Stale male perspiration, pungent woodsmoke, tobacco and whiskey are not perfumes much to my taste. But I suppose if we are venturing into the land of the unwashed we must get used to it.'

'So you won't mind if I smoke?' Bradshaw replied,

taking a sniff at his shirt. 'Yeah, I guess you got a fair point. You forgot to mention the stench of horse sweat.'

'What did happen to your horse?' Lieutenant Page asked, as he poured him a glass of brandy.

'A Sioux shot him.'

'What?' Heather exclaimed. 'On purpose?'

'No. He was aiming at *me*.' He sniffed the shot and tossed a mouthful back. 'Thanks, pal. Best of luck.'

'You had a run-in with the Sioux?' Captain Marsh asked. 'Who were they?'

'Minneconjou. Three of 'em.'

'What happened?'

'I killed 'em.'

'You killed them?' Heather, a liberal Easterner, was even more indignant. 'Was that necessary? Or do you get a thrill out of killing Indians:'

Brad tamped down his pipe and lit up.

'Waal, missy,' he drawled, 'iffen you was robbed of all your belongings, stripped naked and told to run for your life – which is quite a fanciful thought – what would you do?'

Aunt Maud snorted with indignation.

'Really! What an uncouth thing to say.'

'It was the young lady who asked the question. I can assure you I don't get a thrill out of killing Indians. Only the thrill of being still alive. I had no other choice. Luckily I had my Spencer tucked away.'

'What's your handle, mister?' the pot-bellied Captain Marsh demanded, as he, too, lit his pipe.

25

'Bradshaw.' The stranger scratched at his growth of stubble and grinned ruefully at the girl. 'You can call me Brad.'

'Hey,' Marsh exclaimed, 'you ain't the one they call Lonesome Bradshaw? I've heard about you, how you was one of the first to lead hunting-parties up into the Yellowstone. Weren't you chief scout to Custer when he went into the Black Hills?'

'Yeah, that's me. That's what stirred up all the trouble, him claiming there was gold glinting through the grass. He allus was a loudmouth.'

'Are you speaking of General Custer?' Aunt Maud shrieked. 'Our nation's hero?'

Brad knocked back the shot. 'For a start he weren't general. He was Loo-tenant Colonel. I ain't doubting his courage, but he was an undisciplined hothead. It was his own fault he died at the Little Big Horn and took two hundred and twenty-five brave men to their deaths with him. Personally, I think it's just as well he did die, otherwise he'd probably be standing right now as president and America would have another warmonger at the helm.'

'What?' Lieutenant Page protested. 'That's blasphemy, sir.'

'Call it what you like.' Brad's grey eyes glimmered malevolently through their slits. 'There's a thing called free speech in this country and that's my personal opinion.'

'That's as maybe.' Aunt Maud flapped her hand dismissively. 'But, more to the point, are you saying

26

there are still marauding Indians out there? I under-
stood they had all been paciified.'

'Not all. A few got through the army dragnet. Why,
lady, what's your concern? Where you headed?'

'If it's any business of yours, which it isn't,' Aunt
Maud said as she patted a brooch at the throat of her
modest grey dress, 'my ward and I are disembarking
at Miles City, and, after we have seen our lawyer, a Mr
Horniblow, we plan to take possession of the
Diamond Square ranch on the Powder River.'

It was the turn of Brad to look drop-jawed.

'You what?'

Heather butted in to explain.

'Mr Robert Henshall was my uncle. He apparently
had no other kin, and consequently the ranch goes
to me.'

'To you? What, you mean he has died?'

'He was killed,' Captain Marsh explained with some
vehemence. 'Him an' his foreman, shot in the back by
some sneakin' rustlers, or maybe even redskins.'

'Hell, this is news to me,' Brad muttered. 'I only
got a letter from him a week ago. Look,' he pulled it
from his shirt pocket, 'he offered me a job as foreman at a hundred a month. That's where I was
headed when them Minneconjou jumped me.'

Aunt Maud snatched the missive from him and
raised her lorgnette above her disdainfully pointed
nose.

'Ridiculous!' she snapped. 'You needn't get any
funny ideas that this holds us to anything. A hundred

a month, indeed! Other men are quite happy with thirty.'

Brad took the letter back and tucked it away.

'Don't worry, lady, I wouldn't want to hold you to it. In fact, I wouldn't want to hold you, full stop. Or work for a mealy-mouthed old broiler like you.'

Lieutenant Page gave a gasp of laughter and hastily cupped his hand to his mouth. Recovering, he said sternly:

'Really, sir, that's going too far.'

'Yeah, I'm sorry. I take it back,' Brad said, with a sigh, getting to his feet. 'I ain't aiming to fight a duel over her. She got me mad, that's all. I'll wish you good-night.'

'No need to be so hasty,' Heather cried, tugging at his sleeve. 'My aunt meant no harm. I think we should pay you a month's salary for the waste of your time. Or, perhaps, why don't you come and work the ranch for us?'

'Sorry, miss, I don't work for wimmin.' Brad sat down as Lieutenant Page offered the brandy-bottle again. 'That's my policy. Once bitten twice shy.'

'Good!' the old woman gave a snort of contempt. 'It's absurd. What are you talking about, Heather? I have no intention of running any ranch. Not after what we've just heard about Indians on the warpath. We will sell up for the best price and get back as soon as we can to Boston.'

'I don't know.' Heather made a grimace of her lips. 'What will *you* do, Mr Bradshaw?'

'Me? I'm planning to do the Tennessee two-step with you. So, why don't somebody start up the music?'

'No, seriously,' she protested.

'Waal, seeing as he was a good friend of mine I aim to go take a look around. I'd like to find out just who these back-shooters were. Or who was behind 'em.'

'I got to get back to the bridge,' Captain Marsh bellowed. 'The boy's hangin' on to the wheel. It's a straight run from here on. We'll be anchoring at Fort Buford by morning. Enjoy yourselves, folks.'

Young Page had tired of the talk and had begun pounding away at the piano with his version of 'The Girl I Left Behind Me'.

'How about it?' Brad asked, standing to offer his hand to Heather, and she smiled as, before her aunt could object, she was swept away, trying to avoid the frontiersman's clomping boots.

'I'm a tad outa practice,' he apologized. 'It's the first time I've held a gal in my arms for a couple of months, but I must admit it's kinda pleasant.'

'Hold on!' Lieutenant Page called after a couple of dances. 'I'm not allowing you to monopolize this young lady for the rest of the night.' He disappeared and returned with the stoker and his squeezebox. 'Swing it,' he shouted. 'We're going to make the boards bounce.'

'Waal, I guess I gotta surrender you to this eager young pup,' Brad grudgingly agreed.

'Why don't you dance with her auntie?'

29

'You jokin'?'

Aunt Maud frowned at them, gathering her shawl around her.

'At least you've made a more suitable choice, Heather. I am retiring to our cabin. I'll expect you to join me in at most half an hour.'

But it was two hours later that, with a certain amount of giggling, Heather was escorted back by the two men. She said her good-nights and found Maud snoring in her nightcap in her bunk. She listened to the stalwart frontiersman hefting Claud into his cabin, dumping him on the bed, and pulling off his boots.

'Sleep tight,' he bade him, and clomped away, a little unsteadily, back to his cheaper compartment on the lower deck.

The timbers creaked, the bow thudded into the fast water, and all night the engine reverberated carrying them on their way. By dawn Captain Marsh was unloading military supplies and equipment on the quayside of the settlement on the east side of the Missouri, Fort Buford, taking on more passengers, and heading back towards the mouth of the Yellowstone.

Lieutenant Page cheered and jeered as they passed a fellow officer standing on the bridge of the *Star of the Plain* which was making heavy weather of getting to Fort Buford.

'That's a hundred dollars you owe me,' he shouted.

'It's in the bag,' the captain said, looking forward to his own fifty, and guiding the steamship up through the boisterous Yellowstone floodwaters, past the old Stanley's Stockade and Glendive. 'We'll soon be in Miles City.'

When Heather and her aunt appeared on deck they were passing a mile-wide shallow estuary on the south bank.

'That's the Powder,' Brad went to stand beside them at the rail. 'Fine country, ain't it?'

'Do you think you could guide us to the ranch?' Heather asked.

'I dunno.' He shrugged. 'I'll be around.'

'What are you saying?' Aunt Maud chided her as he ambled away to retrieve his saddle and guns. 'He's the last person I want with us. Heather, it's positively indecent the way you've been throwing yourself at that . . . that desperado. That's no way for a young lady to behave.'

THREE

Milestown, or Miles City as it was now proudly known, was named after General Nelson Miles, and was situated at the confluence of the Yellowstone and the fast-flowing Tongue rivers. It had, a few years before, been just a collection of shacks. But now, in 1880, it had boomed into a rumbustious cowtown and was reknowned as 'the hottest spot on the cold northern plains'.

The criss-crossing streets and alleys boasted not only the Cosmopolitan Theatre, the Grand Central Hotel, Bill Reece's dance-hall, and, the latest fad, a roller-skating-rink, but also saloons, hardware stores, liveries, a gunshop and the Wells Fargo Bank. A warren of red-light parlour-houses had accumulated to slake the lusts of randy cowhands, soldiers from nearby Fort Keogh, buffalo-killers, teamsters, gamblers, and general riff-raff attracted like moths to the flame.

The rickety quayside was stacked high with thousands of buffalo hides awaiting shipment as *The Far West*, its steam-whistle bellowing, manoeuvred in to tie up alongside several other such vessels. This was the hey-day of the paddle steamer, although soon its death-knell would be sounded by the arrival of the railroad.

Brad was one of the first down the gangplank, his saddle on his shoulder. He had no wish to be tied to the skirts of two females, pleasant as one might be. He needed to buy himself a horse, cinch up, and be on his way. But, after calling in at Ringer and Johnson's stables and picking out a nice chestnut, he made his way along the raised wooden sidewalk of the muddy Main Street to a cabin with barred windows that announced itself to be the 'Jail and Law Office'.

'How can I help you, stranger?' A man even taller and broader than Brad was ensconced on a swivel-chair before a roll-top desk, attired in a muddy suit and boots, a gold watch-chain across his protuberant belly and a tin star affixed to his vest. 'You got a worried look. What's your trouble?'

'The Diamond Square ranch on the Powder. That's my problem. I'm told the rancher, Rob Henshall, got gunned down out there a while back. You arrested anybody?'

'Why, what's that to you?'

Bradshaw explained he was a friend from way back, and the lawman introduced himself as Xerces Biedler. 'Jest call me X, everybody else does.' He took

33

a bite at a plug of tobacco and it bulged his cheek as he chawed and relaxed in the chair. 'Well, I guess I can confide in you, mister. I've made my investigations but the trail's gone cold. Anybody could have taken a shot at him. There's been trouble between him and his neighbours, a bunch of greasers who run the Topaz spread on Mizpah Creek. They're my main suspects, but as yet I cain't prove it.'

'What are their names?'

'The del Toros. There's the old man, Antonio, but he's more or less a cripple. He's got a crazy daughter, wilder than any buckaroo, Euala she's called. She dresses in cowboy clothes and is as trigger-happy as any drunken *vaquero*. She more or less runs the place. I'd stay out of her way if I were you.'

'Anybody else to avoid?' Brad gave his sarcastic, thin-lipped, smile. 'Have you questioned these people, Biedler?'

'Sure I have. There's her brother, a young ne'er-do-well, Rodrigo. I had him in here and softened him up with my billy-stick. He cried like a baby but he wouldn't admit anything. Euala sure was mad when she came to collect him. If she weren't a female – well, kind of – I'd have damn well shot her.'

'Anybody else who might have had designs on the Diamond Square spread?'

'Hell, man, all you foreigners coming up here – where'd you say you're from? Kansas? – Texans, Mexicans, scum from Missouri driving their herds up here fighting for a piece of the action, trying to get their hands on free government range, anybody could have done it. Rustlers, lariat Indians, how the hell do I know? There's hundreds who could have had their envious eyes on that piece of prime land.'

'Has anybody made a move to take it over? Rob's been dead awhile.'

'Not that I know of.' The sheriff spat a gob of brown juice at a corner spittoon. 'The place has been put in escrow while a relative is located. The Topaz gal reckons she's keeping an eye on the cattle, but I shouldn't be surprised if that ain't a blind just to run most of 'em off for herself.'

'You sound as if you don't like this family, X? You got anything against Mexicans?'

'Nope, not in general. But this lot' – he made a ripping motion with his thumb across his throat – 'Yeuch! A nest of rats. They need clearing out. You'll find her spineless brother over at the Steamboat saloon. He fancies himself as a gambler although I've got my suspicions about that, too.'

'Right, maybe I'll go sound him out. See you, Sheriff.'

Biedler laughed, raucously. 'Don't do anything with that six-shooter that I'd like to do. I might have to string you up. This is a law-abiding town.'

'Yeah? You coulda fooled me.'

Brad's next stop was the office of the attorney-at-law, Mr Charles Horniblow. But his po-faced secretary at the desk told him he would have to wait as the lawyer

THE TALL STRANGER

was in consultation. Brad didn't mean to eavesdrop but the pine-plank walls were thin and he could hear a shrill harridan voice. Could it be Aunt Maud? 'My niece is only twenty. She is legally too young to inherit. I will sign all the papers and act as her ward. As soon as the deeds of the place are passed to me I will be putting it up for sale.'

'In that case,' he heard a deeper man's voice say, 'we can do business.'

It was indeed Aunt Maud and she looked startled when she saw Bradshaw in the lawyer's office as she stepped out to reception. She had a feathered hat, its spotted veil covering her upper face, which was no hardship for him, Brad thought. She pulled her travelling cloak tight and poked a parasol at him.

'Out of my way, man.'

Brad let her pass, with a flicker of a grin, and ignored the lawyer's outstretched hand.

'I don't shake with a man until I've gotten to know him,' he grunted.

'Very wise.' Horniblow rubbed his hands unctuously. He, too, was a thickset, big man, at a time when the average height was about five-feet-six. 'How can I help you?'

'You can help me by laying it on the line. Just what's going on with the Diamond Square place?'

'What exactly is your interest?'

'Maybe I should ask you that question?'

'Oh, yeah? Well, listen, mister, I can't discuss a client's affairs with any Tom, Dick or Harry.'

Horniblow drew himself up and flexed his biceps beneath his suit. 'So, unless you've got any claim on the estate I'd ask you to get out of my office. Pronto.'

'I happen to have had a chat with Miss Heather Monro only last night and she told me she was over twenty-one and planning on running the Diamond Square as a ranch. How about that?'

'No, she must have been trying to impress you. I have it on good authority that she is under age. The lady you just met will be selling the ranch.'

'To you, maybe?'

'To the highest bidder. Goodbye, Mr Bradshaw. If you'll excuse me, I'm a busy man.'

'Me, too. So long.'

The Steamboat Palace had been built with salvage lumber from the *S.S. Yellowstone* wrecked at Buffalo Rapids a few years before – consequently it was a curiously-shaped dive. Heavy oak timbers had been hauled into town and log walls built around their curved configurations so the saloon had the look and feel of being inside a steamboat cabin. At least, what could be seen of it through a haze of smoke from cigars and noxious whale-oil lanterns.

'Gimme whiskey,' Scarface Jack Mosby hollered at the liquor-dispenser, Sam Rollins. 'I got me a thirst.'

Rollins, his heavy mustachios making up for the fact that he was as bald as a billiard ball, plonked a tumbler before the ruffian and filled it to the brim.

'I hear somebody's been asking questions,' he said.

'Yeah, some dude name of Bradshaw. New in town. I'm keeping an eye on him, don't worry.' Jack had to shout above the hullabaloo for the bar was packed with a mass of humanity, rough-looking men and rouged, skimpily attired 'prairie nymphs'. He stood, his fists spread-eagled on the bar, and took in the spectacle of spinning roulette wheels, games of monte, keno and poker in progress at the green baize tables. 'He ain't nothin' I can't take care of.'

Rollins, in his shirt-sleeves and celluloid collar, eyed him, dubiously.

'I hope so. I wish I'd never heard of Rob Henshall.'

'Don't go gettin' cold feet and blabbin' your mouth off.' The lanky Scarface Jack had half of his scalp lost to a Cheyenne's knife. The skin had grown back, wrinkled and red. The Cheyenne had not survived. 'I'll be keepin' an eye on you, too,' he growled.

'It weren't nothin' to do with me. I didn't want that.'

'We're all part of it, so shut up.' Angrily, Jack hurled the half-finished whiskey in its tumbler at the log fire. It exploded with a *whoomp* of broken glass. 'Gimme another,' he yelled.

Lonesome Bradshaw had had a cut-throat shave at the barber-shop and soaked in a barrel of hot suds at the back. He had bought a clean shirt, underwear, pants and socks and discarded his used ones in a pile. Clean-scrubbed and dressed, his six-gun cinched on his hip, he felt like a new man.

The mud sucked at his boots as he clambered through the traffic of horses and buggies. A line of sullen, steaming bulls stood abandoned with their double wagon-load of sacks of flour and casks of whiskey. They had hauled it all the way from Fort Laramie. But, as soon as he reached town, the bull-whacker had dived off to 'pickle his onions', as they say, amid the calico queens of the infamous Cottage Saloon.

Brad spotted the Steamboat Palace and pushed through the swinging doors and the drinkers and gamblers. He peered around him through narrowed lids and nudged an old-timer.

'I'm looking for Rodrigo del Toro. Any idea?'

The hairy-jawed oldster winked and grinned toothless gums.

'He be over there, mister. He ain't often no place else. I'm warnin' you, he's sharp with the deck. Don't trust the varmint.'

Brad slapped his shoulder and looked across to a corner where a game was in progress. A young Mexican, handsome in a weak-chinned way, a mass of black curls hanging down over his tanned brow and narrow face, was seated with his back to the wall. He was dealing the pack. He was neatly, if flamboyantly attired in a white embroidered shirt and black velvet pants. There was a double gun belt around his waist. Maybe he fancied himself as a shootist as well as gambler.

'What's your affliction, stranger?' Sam Rollins asked, surlily.

'How about one of them Milwaukee lager beers you got advertised outside.'

Rollins filled a foaming tankard and slid it to him.

'That's fifty cents. The celebrated Falk's and Schlitz's lager. Genuine German. Nothing but the best in this establishment.'

'You the owner of this joint?' Brad took a draught of the ale and watched Rollins as he seemed to wince and hesitate.

'Not any longer. Got into financial difficulties and some fella bought me out. I'm just the barkeep now.'

'What fella?'

'What's it to you? What's with all the questions? What you doing in town, yourself?'

'Yeah,' Scarface Jack snarled, butting in. 'It ain't healthy or wise to go round asking stoopid questions in these parts, mister. Get my drift?'

Brad turned and faced Jack, watching him through his eye-slits across the top of the glass as he drained the beer in one.

'It would be difficult not to.' He pushed the glass away and flipped down fifty cents. 'But maybe I should warn you I don't like threats.'

He turned on his heel and pushed through the crowds of men hung over the tables, their unwashed

body-odour mingling with that of the doxies' cheap
perfume.

'Howdy,' he said, nodding to the men playing
poker in the corner. 'Mind if I sit in?'

Rodrigo del Toro looked up and his lips curled
back over white teeth in a flashing, contemptuous
smile.

'If you got the money, mister, I got the time to take
it off you.'

Brad took a roll of greenbacks from his shirt
pocket, peeled off a dollar and tossed it into the pot.
'You're the dealer, I take it.'

'Thass right.' Rodrigo flickered a wink at one of
the men and began to do just that, dealing with
nimble fingers. 'Right, let's play.'

Brad studied his hand. It was nothing to write
home about, even if he had a home to write to. The
same occurred over and over again, while the
Mexican youth somehow came up with kings and
queens and aces with curious regularity. Brad's bank
roll got alarmingly lighter.

'You win again,' he sighed. 'I hear tell your daddy
runs the Topaz ranch. Don't you ever do any work
out there? Or do you spend your whole life in here?'

Rodrigo detected a sour note to the stranger's
tone and he gave a scoffing grin.

'What I do with my life is my affair, mister. If you
don't like losing you are free to get up and go.'

'You figure it ain't my lucky day?' Lonesome
Bradshaw gently touched a corner of a card with his

finger and thumb detecting a roughness to it. 'I'm getting up but I'm taking twenty-six dollars with me. That's what I've lost so far when maybe I might have been winning.'

Rodrigo tensed, pushing his chair back, his hands reaching back towards his guns.

'Those are dangerous words.'

'I'll take my losses back,' Brad said in a slow, deliberate tone, 'and we'll say no more.' He began to count out dollars from the pile in the table centre, but looked up. 'Unless you've any objection.'

'Sure I have objection,' Rodrigo hissed out. 'What you saying, mister?'

'I'm saying these cards are marked.' Brad's voice was louder and more aggressive now and the noisy saloon suddenly fell hushed as the men around the table tried to draw back out of the line of possible gunfire. 'I'm saying you're a lousy lowdown cheatin' rattlesnake. That's what I'm saying, son. Could I put it any clearer?'

'You're a liar.' A startled look in his eyes, Rodrigo suddenly went for the pearl-handled Smith & Wessons on his hips. But Brad was up before him, hurling the table over and knocking the Mexican back against the wall. One of Rodrigo's revolvers exploded, the slug smashing into the table, as he lost his balance and tumbled to one side over his chair. Bradshaw jumped to grab him before he could recover and smashed his right fist into his jaw, He hauled him up by his shirt and gave him another piledriver. Rodrigo went down on his back but tried to fire his right-hand weapon again. Brad stamped on his wrist and kicked the Smith & Wesson away.

'You don't seem to learn.' He hefted the youth to his feet by his torn shirt and punched him a hard jab in his solar plexus making him double up and gasp. Brad's knee made contact with his nose and blood spurted as the youth tumbled back. 'You had enough? You try those tricks you better be faster next time.'

He bent and took the left-hand Smith & Wesson from its holster, spun the cylinder and emptied the bullets, which rolled across the floor. He tossed it back at Rodrigo and picked up the pack of cards, patted them neat and put them in his pocket with his recovered dollars.

'I'll keep these.'

'Sure, you're purty good, aincha, beating up a stoopid punk greaser kid?' Scarface Jack gave a roar of laughter, leering at Bradshaw from the bar. 'But are you fast enough for me?' With drunken bravado he hauled a Colt .45 from his belt and sent a shot whistling past Bradshaw's head. 'Take that, you—'

Before he could finish his sentence he howled as the Kansan drifter's lead smashed across his forearm. He dropped the gun and went down on one knee hugging his wrist.

'Don't shoot. Don't kill me!' he cried out.

Brad stepped towards him, threateningly, his Remington aimed in readiness as Scarface whined:

'I was only kiddin' when I took a pot at you. I didn't hit you, *did* I?'

'No, he's too drunk to know what he's doing.' The barkeep reached for a shotgun. 'You can't shoot a drunk.'

'Put that away, 'Brad growled, 'or you'll be included, too.'

He kicked the Colt spinning away, relieved Jack of a throwing-knife, which he thudded into a wall, hauled him to his feet, then went and collared the dazed Rodrigo who was coming round, feeling at his jaw. He collected them both.

'Git moving,' he drawled, prodding them with the Remington. 'I'm making a citizen's arrest.'

'Good for you, stranger,' the old-timer wheezed. 'Nifty shootin'. Them two's been ruling the roost in here for far too long.'

Brad pushed the two delinquents out of the batwing doors and forced them to struggle at gunpoint along through the mud of the main street as onlookers watched from the sidewalks.

Sheriff Biedler came from the door of his office.

'What's going on?' he roared.

Scarface Jack began loudly protesting his innocence until Bradshaw buffaloed him across the back of his neck with his revolver butt and he went slithering in the mud.

'You ruffian!' Aunt Maud and Heather were among the watchers. 'What are you doing to those poor men? Didn't you see him, Sheriff? He attacked that injured man. Look at all the blood on both of them. Aren't you going to arrest him?'

Biedler glanced at her and sent a squirt of tobacco juice to land close to her buttoned bootees.

'I'll take care of this, lady, without your help. Bring 'em in here, mister. What's your complaint?'

Brad shoved them into the jailhouse and a vacant cell. The sheriff slammed the door on the miscreants.

'This young un' thought he could swindle me using a marked deck. Here,' he produced the weighted deck from his shirt-pocket, 'it's cleverly disguised. Feel the corner of that ace of spades. The other one attempted to murder me when I objected.'

'I was only joking,' Scarface whined. 'I've told you.'

'Attempted homicide and cheatin' at cards.' The sheriff took another bite of tobacco and studied the cards as he chewed. 'Them are hangin' offences in this territory. Good thang I got my new rope ready. I been looking forward to christening it. I'll put 'em up 'fore the judge in the mornin'.'

'Good,' Brad said, as the lock was turned and, swinging his keys, the sheriff stepped out on to the sidewalk with him. 'But maybe that's a bit harsh? Six months breaking rocks might be a better sentence.'

'No, that only hardens 'em. Hang 'em high, I say.'

'Yeah, well, I'll see you in court in the morning.'

Brad strolled away along to the hotel. He could smell vittles cooking. The little ruckus had given him quite an appetite. He seated himself in the dining-room and was just about to tuck into a steaming plate of tenderloin-and-carrot casserole when Aunt Maud and her niece came in. Brad stood and raised a hand to the girl.

'Heather, could I have a word?'

'How dare you accost us. Really!' Maud looked about ready to hit him with her parasol. 'Heather, you're not going to have anything to do with this desperado?'

'Go and find yourself a table, Aunt. I won't be long.'

'Really!' the old girl shrieked again as she strutted away.

'*Really* seems to be her favourite word.'

'My aunt doesn't seem to find much right with the world. What did you want, Brad?'

'I was wondering. You said you were over twenty-one. Your aunt claims you ain't.'

'But, of course I am.' The girl smiled. 'I brought my birth certificate along to prove it.'

'Where is it?'

'I gave it to Maud. She said she needed to show it to Mr Horniblow.'

'That's different to what I heard.'

'Perhaps you misunderstood. Although I don't quite see why you—'

'You think it's none of my business? Waal, I got the feeling Horniblow's as crooked as a wolf's hindleg. But what lawyer ain't? I'll go see him in the morning,

46

sort it out. Huccome you've got such a miserable old buzzard like her as a relative?'

Heather smiled again at the simile.

'To tell you the truth she's not really my aunt. More of a nanny. She looked after me as a child and my father until he died. She sort of appointed herself aunt. I mean, I can't just tell her I don't need her around any more.'

'Maybe you'll have to. It strikes me she's after lining her own pockets. Then it might well be *her* who tells *you* to pack your bags.'

'Don't be ridiculous. Where on earth do you get these crazy ideas from? I wish you wouldn't say those sorts of things. And, tell me, was it necessary to beat up those two men?'

'Waal!' Brad gave a gasp of exasperation. 'They had both just tried to shoot me so I felt I had to do somethang with the lousy polecats.'

'I see.' Heather looked hurt and concerned as she rose. 'I'll try to explain that to Maud. I'll leave you to your dinner. Good-night, Mr Bradshaw.'

Brad watched her flounce away to join her aunt, her bustle swaying beneath her satin dress.

'Goodnight,' he muttered, returning to his food. 'But maybe not goodbye.'

FOUR

'Hai—yagh!' Euala del Toro quirted her black stallion, Diablo, from side to side, as she galloped him across the military bridge slung on pine-pole supports across the tempestuous Tongue River. Her shining black tresses streamed out from beneath a hard-brimmed Mexican hat and she was dressed and rode astride like a man. Her silk blouse and bandanna, fringed jacket and buckskin chaps gave her the look of some wild *vaquero* rather than a girl of nineteen.

'Whoah,' she shouted as she hauled the horse in outside the courthouse.

The big and brawny Sheriff X. Biedler was leading his chained prisoners who looked a tad sorry for themselves, towards the log cabin that served as courthouse.

'It looks like I got here just in time,' she cried.

'Keep outa this, Euala,' Biedler shouted, cocking his rifle in her direction.

'What are you doing with my brother?'

'What'n hell's it look like? He's up on a charge of cheating at cards. A hanging offence.'

'Who says he did?' the girl asked, pointing a black-gloved finger at Bradshaw. 'Him?'

'He tried to rook me of my cash with a marked deck,' Bradshaw said. 'He's gotta learn that ain't right.'

'I didn't do it, Sis,' Rodrigo called out, plaintively. 'Stop 'em. Don't let 'em do this. I'm innocent, I swear.'

'Me, too,' Scarface Jack wailed, grinning at her as he threw his cuffed wrists into the air. 'Look what he done to me. I nearly bled to death. What will my poor old mother say? This is gonna break her heart.'

'Who gave you the right to accuse my brother?' Euala spurred her stallion towards Bradshaw and without warning slashed her bone-handled riding-quirt, with its knotted leather thong, across his face.

He instinctively stepped back a pace from the spirited, stomping stallion, thus evading the worst of the blow, but the whip-end cut across his face.

'Try that again,' he growled.

'Take that!' The girl raised her arm again and snapped the whip at him, but this time he snatched at it, gave it a jerk and hauled her from the screaming horse. She tumbled down and Brad held her upright, then backhanded her across her jaw sending her spinning into the mud. Euala lay there, staring at him, speechless, rubbing her cheek, her dark eyes seething with hatred.

'Look at him! He's doing it again!' Aunt Maud was among the bystanders. 'This time he's beating a girl. Oh, the unspeakable oaf!'

Brad wiped the blood-streak from his cheek.

'A gal, is she? There was me thinking she was a guy.' His lips flickered in a crooked smile. 'Waal, she deserved it, whatever sex she is, the wildcat. Anybody who strikes me gits struck back. Maybe it's time she larned that 'fore she goes cracking her whip.'

Euala got to her booted feet, retrieved her angry stallion and hitched him to a fence, her cheek smarting from the blow.

'Quiet, boy.'

She turned to Bradshaw. 'So, just what evidence have you got against my brother?' she asked, struggling to control herself.

Brad took the pack from his pocket, presented the ace of spades to her, rubbing its corner.

'Feel that.'

Euala del Toro did so, her face severe. This time she turned on Rodrigo and slashed the quirt at his sleeve.

'You stupid fool,' she shouted in Spanish. 'You think you're a big shot, waste your life in saloons. Look where it's got you.'

'Hey, he's my prisoner.' Brad snatched the quirt from her, broke its carved bone handle across his knee and tossed it away into the mud. 'You're too fond of doing that. He may be your brother but he's got his rights.'

'You cannot hang him,' she shrieked at Biedler. 'I'll kill you if you do.'

'Hangin's too good for him.' The sheriff nonchalantly spat a gob of tobacco juice in her direction. 'Hoss-thieves and card-cheats git the same treatment. Rustlers, too,' he pointed a finger at her, 'you wanna remember that. You might well be next on the list. You greasers gotta learn your place.'

'You sayin' she's a rustler, Sheriff?' Bradshaw asked.

'Maybe I can't prove it yet, but plenty of stock's gone missing from the Henshall place. She's the most likely suspect.'

'Yes, string her up, too,' a scrawny settler woman in the crowd shouted. 'These greasers ain't wanted in these parts.'

'Did I hear somebody say I got hanging business?' A portly little man in a frock-coat, stained silk vest, and crumpled top hat, pushed his way through the throng. 'Is that right, Sheriff?'

'It sure is. Make way for the judge,' Biedler ordered. 'These two felons deserve the full weight of the law.'

'In that case I better have a snort.' His fleshy nose glowing like a red bulb, the judge tipped a silver flask to his lips. 'Puts me in a hanging mood.'

'Just a minute.' Brad was beginning to feel uneasy about this as Euala del Toro spat out a torrent of

Spanish abuse at them. 'Hold on, gal. I'm beginning to think this is a bit hard. You're not seriously thinking of making 'em kick air?'

'Why not?' Biedler beamed. 'Folks like a good hanging. And my rope needs stretching.'

Brad glanced first at Heather in the crowd, then at the fiery Spanish girl, then at the prisoners.

'Ach, forget it,' he snapped. 'I withdraw my complaints against 'em both.'

'You what?' the judge blustered. 'This is a serious waste of my time, mister. I could fine you for contempt of court.'

'We ain't in court yet and just as well by the look of things. I'm not giving evidence so there's nothing you can do. Sorry to disappoint you, ladies and gents.'

'You'd better watch your step, buddy,' Biedler roared, as the tall frontiersman turned and strolled away towards the livery. 'We don't need troublemakers like you in this town.'

Brad gave a contemptuous wave of his hand without turning around.

'It ain't the kind of town I particularly like,' he muttered. 'Hangin' crazy, if you ask me.'

He was in the stable packing his warbag and tying his blanket, rolled around his rifle, behind the saddle, adjusting the bridle and giving a pat to his new chestnut gelding, when Euala del Toro rode into the livery doorway. She swung down from her stallion and walked over to him.

'I guess I owe you an apology,' she said, offering her gloved hand to shake. 'Thank you for saving my brother's life.'

Brad studied her, the carved cheekbones, the full, sensuous lips; detecting, too, a ripeness of movement beneath her silk blouse. 'You really think they would have. . . ?'

'True. The sheriff wants us out of the way. He hates us, the fat pig. If there's any way I can thank you . . '

Brad took her hand in his strong grip and a smile flickered on his lips.

'Waal, I could think of a way.' He pulled her into him tight, twisting her arm behind her back, pressing his mouth so hard on hers he heard her teeth grate as she struggled to push him off.'

'You filthy . . .' she protested as she pulled her mouth free. She broke into a string of vehement Spanish. 'Don't think you—'

But he paid no heed, swung her up, one arm under her kicking legs, carried her back into the stable and tossed her down on to a heap of hay.

'You swine.' Euala lay glowering up at him. 'You wouldn't dare.'

'Wouldn't I?'

The Mexican girl screamed and tried to grab at a pitchfork but he was too quick for her, leaping on her, holding her down in the soft hay, one hand feeling for her breasts beneath her blouse, the other gripping her nape, holding her still while he kissed her again.

Slowly Euala ceased her kicking and screaming, and gloved fingers closed around his shoulders, pulling him tight into her. . . .

'Oh, my God!' Maud squawked as she came into the livery and saw the backwoodsman thrusting apart the girl's kicking, buckskin-chapped legs. 'What's he doing now?'

Heather was behind her and she stopped, frozen like a statue, cupping her hands to her lips, speechless. They had come to hire a buggy but she had not expected a sight like this.

Brad, too, froze for a few seconds, then relaxed and swung up off the girl.

'Howdy,' he said, with a grin. He picked up his hat and brushed himself down. 'I guess you could say she's been saved by the bell.'

'You see now what he's like, the villain. A would-be rapist!'

'Yes,' Heather whispered. 'I thought, at least, he was a gentleman.'

'Well,' Brad replied off-handedly, as he returned to his horse. 'She really needs a good spanking, but I'll have to forgo that pleasure.'

'You. . . .' Euala del Toro was back on her feet, adjusting her hat, haughty as ever. 'You ever try, I'll castrate you.'

'We'll see.' Brad swung up into the saddle and touched his hat to them as he rode out. 'So long, ladies.'

But before leaving town he had one other call to make. He stepped down outside the lawyer's office. It looked like Horniblow had had a late night because he was just coming down from his living-quarters above his office, scratching at his unshaven jaw and yawning.

'What do *you* want?' he growled as his pointy-nosed secretary gave him a mug of coffee and Bradshaw stepped inside.

'I wanna speak to you. What's happened to the birth certificate of the Monro girl?'

'What's that got to do with you?'

'Just answer my question.' Bradshaw shoved him back towards his inner office, spilling the coffee in his hand.

'What the hell are you doing?' The stocky lawyer angrily threw the hot coffee in Bradshaw's face and swung a hefty right to his jaw. Brad was rocked back crashing against the secretary's desk as she screamed and tried to wriggle out of the way. He wiped the coffee from his face and blocked another punch that Horniblow threw at him by raising his left guard. 'Get outa here, you stinking prairie rat.'

'Not 'til I get some answers. Sorry, miss.' Brad eased the girl to one side. 'Just stand over there, will you?' He came back with a swinging chop of his calloused right hand to the lawyer's throat, making him gasp, taking him by surprise. He followed up with a left to his abdomen, but for a pen-pusher he was tougher than Bradshaw had anticipated. Soon the two of them were swapping blows, careeering around the outer office, crashing over desks and chairs and filing-cabinets, cursing and grunting as they fought.

'Got you,' Horniblow cried, as he tried to gouge out Brad's eyes with his thumbs. But, half-blinded, the backwoodsman kneed him sharp in the groin, brought his hands up to break his hold, and put every ounce of muscle he possessed to punch his right fist into the lawyer's face.

'That's what *you* think!'

The lawyer went back-pedalling into his inner office and landed in the waste-paper basket.'That's where you belong, pal.'

'All right.' Horniblow put up his hands, spread-eagled, and with a thumb wiped away blood trickling from his nose. 'This is stupid.' He tried to get to his feet and extricate himself from the wire receptacle clinging to his backside. 'Look at the mess you've made. Are you crazy? Coming in here like a mad bull. I oughta sue you for assault. You mighta broken my nose.'

Brad straightened his bandanna and scraped fingers through his unruly hair.

'I'll rearrange your features and furniture some more if I don't get an answer.'

Horniblow's coarse face split into a grin.

'If you really want to know, it got burned. I was sorting out some unwanted manuscripts last night and I tossed it in by mistake. See, there are the very ashes in this basket. Silly of me, wasn't it?'

'Yeah.' Brad bit back his anger. 'You could say so.'

He picked up his hat and turned on his heel. Outside he swung on to the chestnut.

'He's as crafty as a bag of foxes,' he muttered. 'I've a good idea what him and that old haybag are up to.' He touched spurs to the gelding, which he had named Blaze, and headed out of town, heading across the plain towards the Powder River.

FIVE

God's own country, they called it, the hundreds of square miles of fine grazing land south of the Yellowstone River. Only four years before it had still been the realm of 20,000 Sioux and Cheyenne and millions of buffalo. But the Indians had been deposed, hunted down and blown to atoms by the army's howitzers, or herded on to the reservations, the northern buffalo herds decimated. The plains straddling the Wyoming–Montana border were up for grabs, first come first served, white men arriving from far and wide, staking their claims to the open range and enforcing their boundaries at gunpoint. To conform to some manner of legality they would take an advertisement in the *Yellowstone Journal* announcing that they had taken possession of a tract of land. Generally, in this free-for-all, such claims were accepted. Possessory rights, they called them.

One of the finest stretches of water and grass was the Powder River country where Rob Henshall had staked out his territory, built his ranch house with his own hands from hillside timber, and stocked his spread with longhorns he and his cowboys herded up from Kansas.

It was a tough, lonesome life but he and his wife, Alice, seemed hardy enough to face the rigors of long winters when sub-zero arctic blizzards swept across the land. Rob knew that covetous eyes were on his herd and his land but he had thought himself up to driving off those human coyotes. A hard man, older by sixteen years than Brad, he had survived the internecine fighting of the Kansas–Missouri border raids in the big war, when neighbour slaughtered neighbour. Brad knew from his occasional letters that he had hoped to find peace and prosperity in this new land. But, maybe after the death of his wife and baby he had lost heart and things had started to slide. And then a backshooter's bullet had got him. But who had fired it was anybody's guess.

Brad rode all morning across the rolling plains where after the snowmelt the grass was beginning to green over. He saw no humans except for gangs of buffalo-hunters about their grisly trade. They would take only the robes, sometimes hoofs and horns, leaving the red-raw carcasses to rot. The reason for their stinking industry was simple: greed. They could get four dollars a hide. If they shot fifty to a hundred in a day that was well-paid work.

It was late in the afternoon by the time he sighted the Powder. He sat his horse on a bluff and looked along its sun-glistening, wide meanders. Sheltered by a clump of cottonwoods beneath a cliff of pines was the log ranch house with its surrounding corrals and outbuildings. A trickle of blue woodsmoke rose from a tin chimney but there didn't seem to be a lot of activity. And he had only encountered a few clumps of cattle in the vicinity. Rob had been dead a month. So in that time, rustlers must have taken the opportunity to run off most of the herd.

He let his horse drink at the riverside, then nosed him along through the cottonwoods. The ranch house was not a pretty sight. It looked run-down, neglected and deserted. There were broken windows and stable doors, creaking on their hinges, banging forlornly in the harsh prairie wind. There were weeds knee-high on the porch and a garden table and chairs, where Rob and his wife might have sat to admire the summer sunsets, were overturned. The front door was solid and locked. Brad peered through a lace-curtained window and saw a kangaroo rat in the kitchen nosing into a sack of flour. They were lucky that human rats hadn't taken over the house by now.

The smoke was coming from the low-slung log bunkhouse. It was only four o'clock so he did not expect to see anyone in there. He loosened the Remington revolver in its holster just in case there might be any possibly unfriendly, varmints.

'Anybody at home,' he shouted and kicked at the door with his boot. 'I'm coming on in.'

He waited a few seconds. Gradually the door was eased open a foot and a surly-looking cow-puncher, his hair tousled, sleep in his eyes, poked his head out.

'Yeah, whadda ya want?'

'Just making a social call,' Brad replied. 'I could kill for a cup of cawfee.'

'No need to do that. There's one on the stove and some Mulligan stew free to all who's hungry. Come on in, mister.'

'I was a friend of Rob Henshall. I was already on my way up here when I heard the sad news,' he said as he stepped into the fusty gloom. It smelt as though a pack of polecats was bunked down. That epithet could be freely applied to the five men who sat around on their cots, which were strategically placed around the stove. Three appeared to be playing with a pack of greasy cards, while the other two were still blanketed in their pits. Unwashed, uncombed, in their crumpled range-clothes, all looked as though they had been pulled through a thornbush backwards.

When he had helped himself from the jug of thick black coffee, and been introduced to the men, Brad drawled:

'Looks to me like this place has gone to the devil. Shouldn't you boys be out on the range tending to the herd, or at least mending that corral fence?'

'Are you joking?' The one called Rusty, who had invited him in and seemed to be the leader of the bunch, made a down-turned grimace and shrugged.

61

'We ain't been paid for a month. Maybe we won't be for another month. Nobody's gonna work for fresh air.'

'Where's all the cattle gone?'

'Your guess is as good as ours,' a bearded one in the bed drawled. 'What's it to you, stranger?'

'Just that Rob was a good friend of mine and I don't like to see this place going to rack and ruin. I figure it's about time y'all got up offen your butts.'

'Don't come giving us orders, pal,' Danny Murphy the bearded one, aggressively responded. 'It's bad enough with that Mex bitch from the Topaz coming over here, poking her nose in and cracking her whip.'

Brad gave a cracked laugh as he sipped at his coffee.

'She don't seem to have had much success if her aim was to whip you out on the range. Maybe she goes about it the wrong way?'

'Yeah, she's so full of herself,' Rusty agreed, sitting on his bunk and shuffling the pack impatiently. 'Going on about how the spring round-up's coming and we ought to be cutting out our cows from hers. It's not as if she's paying us. She just wants us to help for free.'

Brad tipped his hat over his eye and scratched the back of his head.

'That sounds a good idea to me.'

'I tell you again, it ain't. Not unless there's cash at the end coming to us.'

'Well, Rusty, that's your entitlement, I guess, but personally I'd go crazy with shack fever sitting around here doing sod-all all day.' Brad got to his feet and poked his nose into the stewpot on the stove. It had a very gamey aroma, probably had been bubbling for weeks. 'I *will* try a plate of Mulligan.' He found a tin dish and spoon. 'Man's gotta keep his strength up. Maybe I'll be lucky if it don't kill me. Then I think I'll go over take a look at this Mex bitch, as you call her. She's over at Mizpah Creek, ain't she? How do I get there?'

'Follow the river south to the next confluent,' Rusty said. 'That's the Mizpah stream. You'd better have a white flag ready to wave. Some of those *vaqueros* are quick on the trigger. They might take you for a rustler.'

Brad spooned the thick, greasy gravy of onions, beef, liver, kidneys and other unidentifiable, contents of the stew into his mouth.

'Not bad,' he said. 'Could do with a few chilli peppers. So, boys, who do ye think's behind the rustling? Who killed Rob?'

The scruffy cowpokes glanced at each other, apprehensively, a warning in their eyes. 'We ain't got a clue,' Rusty said quickly. 'Him and the ramrodder, Rick, were out on their own. When we found them their bodies were cold.'

'Weren't there any tracks, any sign?'

'There was a blizzard blowing, wasn't there?' Murphy shouted, angrily. 'It wiped out all sign. Jasus, man, the sheriff's already asked us these questions. What are you, another law man?'

'Nope, I'm just planning on getting to the bottom of it.' Brad went and rinsed the plate in a bucket of water on a bench. 'Thanks for the grub, boys. See you later. Don't you go exerting yourselves, mind.'

Outside he poked his head back in. 'Oh, you might be having more visitors. A couple of females, one young and purty, t'other a miserable old termagant with a face like the bottom of a yard broom. They seem to have the idea they'll be selling this place. So you might get your back wages after all.'

Brad strode over to his horse and fed him a handful of splitcorn before swinging aboard again and moving out. He shook his head. 'There sure are some lazy sons-uv-bitches around,' he muttered. 'Serve 'em right if the old faggot tells 'em all to git lost.'

Antonio del Toro had fortified the Topaz ranch, or Triangle T, to give it its brand name, with an encircling stockade of stout lodgepole pines. He had also taken the precaution of covering the windows with iron bars and wooden shutters with ports through which rifles could be poked in case of attack by Sioux or gringos. Sometimes he wondered why he had ever left New Mexico to settle in these cold northern regions, but the grass was good and he had prospered.

Certainly, he had had to fight for his land with his

guns; in an incident at Mizpah Creek he had been ambushed by four bushwhackers and had been blasted in both legs by shotgun scatter at close range. That was two years ago and he had been a virtual cripple since. His attackers had been masked like vigilantes and Antonio had been unable to identify them. The motive was both racist and an attempt to make him quit his ranch. He was lucky, he supposed, that his daughter, Euala, and their *vaqueros*, had arrived and driven the men off, otherwise he might well be dead. Not that it was much of a life, being unable to use his legs.

Antonio was pondering on the events of the past four years since he had arrived with his longhorn herd as he sat in his makeshift wheelchair at the dinner table that evening. His daughter and her brother, Rodrigo, had arrived home shortly before in high dudgeon after riding hard for forty miles across the plains from Miles City.

'That gringo bastard humiliated us,' Rodrigo cried as he pushed his cleared plate away and swallowed the contents of a glass of wine. 'He humiliated me and then he humiliated my sister. He deserves to die.'

'There would have been no trouble if you hadn't brought it upon us.' Euala tossed her dark and shimmering hair back from her face and glowered at him. 'What do you expect a man like that to do if you try to cheat him? He is not one of the sozzle-brained local cowboys. You are lucky he did not kill you.'

'Lucky he did not press charges.' A man attired in black, the clothes tight to his slim body, Mexican-style, spoke. He had grave, dark-eyed features, his nostrils flared as sharp as a hawk's. Raoul Vasconcelos was besotted with Euala, but she would have nothing to do with him in that manner. Foreman of the ranch and an old friend of her father, he had appointed himself her guardian and, whenever possible, followed her everywhere and did her bidding. 'If he *had* Rodrigo, you would this minute have been swinging from their hanging-tree.'

'This man Bradshaw, who is he?' Antonio asked.

'Nobody really knows. He has been a hunter and guide, but apart from that he is a mystery.' Euala touched her cheek which still smarted from the blow he had given her. And she was furious inside still from the way he had treated her like a common whore in the livery stable, throwing her into the hay, trying to have his way with her. She had decided, however, that she had better not mention that incident and incense Rodrigo and Raoul even more. 'He is certainly no gentleman.'

Rodrigo laughed scornfully, his white teeth flashing.

'You must admit you asked for it, slashing your quirt at him as if he was some *peon.*'

'He back-handed you?' Raoul pondered this as if it was incredible. 'If I had been there I would have killed him. If he ever touches you again I will.'

'It's this damned useless son of mine who is the

cause of the trouble.' The father waved a dismissive hand at Rodrigo. 'Like Euala says: she should have been born the man and him the daughter. She is worth a hundred of him.'

Rodrigo jumped to his feet, knocking the glass over.

'Don't speak to me like that, you old fool.'

'If I had my legs in use it would be I who gave you a good thrashing not some gringo. Using marked cards? Pah! You have brought shame on us, on our whole race. Now what will people say of us? That we can't be trusted. How will we get any credit?'

'How the hell do I know?' Rodrigo shouted, throwing his napkin down angrily. 'Or care? I've had enough of you. Don't call me useless. You're the useless one, you cripple.'

'Get out!' Antonio shouted, struggling to get at him, but toppling instead from his chair. 'Get out of my house.'

'Don't worry, I'm going.' Rodrigo pulled his jacket from the chairback, aware that he had said too much, but unable to draw back now. He had gone too far. 'I'll go back to Miles City. At least I have friends there. I can make some money and enjoy life.'

'Who will want to play with a cheat?' Raoul asked.

But Rodrigo was away out of the house, slamming the door, heading for the stable. Euala and Raoul went to help Antonio back into his chair. Then she dashed to the door as Rodrigo rode out through the stable door on a fresh horse.

'Rodrigo, don't! Come back. Apologize to father. It is getting dark. You cannot leave like this.'

But the young Mexican spurred his fiery mount and rode past her, his face grim.

'Open the gate,' he called out to the guard.

'Don't be stupid,' she cried, her words fading away. 'Where will you go. . . ?'

She watched him gallop away towards the hills, a short cut that would take him back down into the winding Mizpah Creek.

'Oh, God,' she whispered. 'Why does he have to be such an idiot?' Her thoughts returned to the tall *Americano* whom, on the spur of the moment, she had slashed with her whip and who had replied in kind: turning the tables on her, in fact. Nobody had ever hit her before. 'I will get even with him,' she vowed. 'Nobody can treat a del Toro like that.'

It was magnificent country. No wonder the Sioux had hung on to it so bitterly. In the Mizpah valley broad expanses of snow-yellowed prairie were broken by isolated buttes and a range of rugged pine-topped hills along the stream which gave sweet, life-sustaining water. Wild, free, dangerous country.

The sun was lowering fast amid reams of golden and silver clouds to the west and Brad began to wonder if it had been wise to go on. He had chosen his horse for the obvious strength of its deep chest and muscled legs, but after near on fifty miles Blaze was beginning to slow and blow hard.

'Maybe we shoulda stayed with them smelly cowpokes overnight,' the rider muttered, scouring the plain for any sign of life. There were cattle, a good many of them, and in fine fettle, too, considering the long winter they had been through. But no sign of human life.

Until, suddenly, round a bend of the creek a Mexican came charging down from the hilltop as if the hounds of hell were after him. Both riders hauled in their mounts, the Mexican swirling a flurry of unmelted snow as he swivelled his mustang on its hindlegs and came back round, a revolver in his hand.

'Rodrigo!' Brad dropped his hand over his own Remington's grip. Slowly, he raised his open fingers in a sign of peace. 'I ain't lookin' for trouble.'

The youth's sombrero had fallen to hang from its cord on his leather-coated back.

'What you want here?' he called, cocking his nickel-plated Smith & Wesson and aiming it at the American.

'I just wanna talk to your family ... about my friend, Rob.'

'Oh, yeah?' Rodrigo sounded doubtful as he spurred his fiery mustang forward. 'You want to try to pin his death on us, too? You need come no further, gringo. I can tell you we had nothing to do with the death of Rob Henshall.'

'I'd like to hear what your father and sister have to

say on that matter.'

'You leave my sister alone, you hear? Or you will die. Now get out of my way. I have—'

A bullet ploughed into Rodrigo's chest, splashing his blood, knocking him off his horse before he could say more. Bradshaw heard the clap of the rifle shot almost simultaneously.

He sprang from his saddle, slapping his horse away, and rolled for cover behind a boulder as another bullet whistled past his own head and the sound of the shot echoed away along the valley. Brad pulled off his hat and held it on top of an adjoining rock. Another blue whistler sent the Stetson flying, showering rock splinters over him and ricocheting onwards.

The marksman, whoever he was, was up on the pine-covered ridge that he had passed. A good half-mile behind him. He saw the flash and powder cloud of another shot and ducked down as the rifle bullet tore past his head.

'Right,' he muttered, pulling free the Spencer slung on his back and taking aim. But the back-shooter was well out of range of a carbine. And his rifle was along with his horse. 'Maybe I'll lie doggo and he'll come lookin'.'

However, as he gritted out the words he heard shooting behind him and looked around to see a bunch of Mexicans heading down from the bluff of pines, the way Rodrigo had come.

'Hell,' he growled. 'They're shooting at *me*!'

He glanced back up to where the marksman had been and saw the dark silhouette of a man on a horse, a rifle in one hand, moving out of the woods and back away over the ridge. So it was safe to get up from that direction. But the oncoming bunch of *vaqueros* didn't look one bit friendly. There was nothing to do but raise himself on to his feet, his Spencer in his hands, and face the new threat.

The leader of the *vaqueros*, he realized, was none other than Euala del Toro and she was screaming and shooting her revolver. Fortunately, the speed and bumpiness of her ride ruined her aim. Nonetheless, her bullets buzzed past him like angry bees. It took a brave man not to take cover or return fire, or, indeed, leap on his horse and run for his life. Brad stood there, the Spencer held across his chest, facing her out. He winced as her last shot nicked his earlobe.

The wild-shooting girl screamed some command in Spanish as she pulled her black stallion to a whinnying halt by her brother's side.

'Why?' she called out, tears welling in her eyes. 'Why did you kill him?'

'I didn't,' he shouted roughly, trying to stay on his feet as two of the Mexicans tossed rawhide lariats over his shoulders, pulling them tight to hold him. He jerked his head back at the hill. 'It was some bastard up there. He musta followed me.'

'What lies do you tell us now?' she shouted, on her knees beside her brother.

One of the Mexicans whom she called Raoul took a look at the wound.

'That is a rifle hole.' He snatched the Spencer from Bradshaw and sniffed the barrel. 'This has not been fired. He did not kill him.'

'He has a rifle, too,' she said.

'That's tucked up in my blanket. You got the wrong man, honey. So maybe you'll tell these stiffs to release me.'

Tears were coursing down Euala's cheeks as she tried to cup Rodrigo's head in her arm and she did not hear him.

'Wait!' she cried. 'He is still breathing. Maybe he has a chance. You men, make a stretcher of your blankets between your horses. We must get him back to the ranch. Gently now. He is losing blood fast.'

'Maybe if you plugged the wound with your bandanna it would help, 'Brad suggested, loosening the lariats and tossing them away.

She looked up at him, scornfully, but tore the youth's shirt open and did what he bid.

'You can come with us,' she said.

'No. I'm going back. I'm going to try to keep up with that shootist,' Brad replied. 'Maybe I'll see you tomorrow, if I'm still alive.'

As he strolled away to catch Blaze the girl called after him, '*Americano*, take care!'

SIX

'Lord have mercy!' Aunt Maud screamed shrilly as she hung on for dear life to the seat of the high-wheeled rig. It bounced, leap-frogged and all but somersaulted down a stomach-churning steep slope as the old-timer, Gary Gibbins, whipped the pair of horses into a break-neck plunge down the ravine towards the Powder River. 'Slow down, you fool! You'll kill us all.'

'Please, Mr Gibbins, pull them in,' Heather pleaded, hanging on to his arm, squashed in as she was on the front seat between the smelly old man and her aunt. 'She didn't mean it.'

'Hech!' Gibbins grinned gummily through his bushy white beard and careered the lightweight buggy down the slope, then set it racing along the flat towards the Diamond Square ranch. 'This'll shake up the old shrew's liver. This'll teach her it ain't wise to talk to me like that.' He turned and winked at Heather. 'Don't you worry, gal. We're all but there.'

Maud had hired him to drive the town's only low-necked carriage, as it was termed, or more aptly, buckboard. Typically, she had nagged him ceaselessly, criticizing his driving ability, his personal hygiene, and his veracity. It was true that he assiduously avoided hot tubs and came out with some tall tales, but when he had stopped to take a snort with some old buff'-hunter cronies and she had told him he was deliberately wasting time, it was the last straw. Maud's head was snapped back so hard she nearly bit off her tongue – which would have been a blessing for all around – as Gibbins howled at the horses and set them into a hair-raising gallop across the plains. It wasn't until he rolled into the ranch environs that he agreed to slow down and pull in.

The horses stood sweating and trembling as Gary climbed down and grinned up at Aunt Maud.

'There, was that fast enough fer ya? Would ya call that wastin' time?'

'You hooligan!' Maud tried to hit him with her parasol and nearly tumbled off her seat. 'You think you're very funny, don't you. Get these bags unloaded and taken into the house.'

'Carry 'em ya-self. Ye got arms an' legs, aincha? I'm only employed to drive.'

By now it was dusk. They had been driving all day and Heather was stiff and weary.

'Oh, please, Mr Gibbins, don't upset her any more,' she stage-whispered. 'I'll give you a hand.'

'Waal, OK,' he grumbled. 'It's only 'cause of you,

missie. Don't she ever stop caterwaulin'? How can ye abide it?'

'Careful how you're handling those bags,' Maud cried as she climbed stiffly down. 'You've got that one upside down.'

'Aw, git knitted.' Bandy-legged and puffing, Gary staggered with a trunk to the front porch as Heather unlocked. 'Howdy, boys,' he shouted, turning to greet the bunch of dishevelled cowpokes who had tumbled from the bunkhouse and came across to see what the commotion was. 'Hope we didn't disturb your slumbers.'

'Howdy.' Rusty stood, thumbs in belt, and nodded at Aunt Maud. 'Who's she?'

'I am the new owner, or we are,' Maud replied shrilly. 'If you men want to keep your jobs you had better jump to it. I want this house swept out, the kitchen tidied and the bed aired. Come on, chop, chop! Tonight, I mean. You' – she prodded the parasol at Murphy – 'Get some wood and get a fire going.'

'We ain't domestics,' he growled. 'We're cowhands.'

'You will do what you're told, my man,' she shrilled. 'Or you will be out of here like a shot.'

But, as she stepped into the house after Heather she shrieked as a rat scuttled out between her open legs and made a beeline for the barn.

'What on earth was that?' she cried, shuddering and shivering and holding her skirts up around her bony, stockinged knees.

'What'd'ja think it was. A rat.' Gary beamed at her. 'Look, thar is another. Quick stamp your boot on his neck.'

Instead, Maud leaped for safety on top of a horse-hair sofa.

'Get them out. Get them all out,' she screamed.

'If you feel somethang nibblin' at your hair in the night you'll know what it is,' Gibbins smirked. 'It certainly won't be me.'

'Lord help me!' Aunt Maud chuntered from her perch. 'Why did I ever come to this Godforsaken place? Why did I ever leave Boston?'

'Calm down, Aunt,' Heather soothed. 'It's not so bad. We'll have the place shipshape in no time.' She had found a witch's-style broom and started vigorously sweeping dust out of the door.

Gibbins helped, hauling rotting sacks of flour away and tidying up. 'You should give that broom to her,' he cackled. 'It'd suit her. She might fly away.'

They had set out from Miles City, accompanied by Sheriff Biedler, who said that due to the threat from Indians they needed protection on the journey. He had Scarface Jack along for company.

'But isn't that disreputable-looking man a criminal?' Heather objected.

'Not really,' Biedler assured her. 'He gets a tad obstreperous when he's whiskied-up. When he's sober he's good to have along in a fight. A well-respected frontiersman. Anyway, he's all I got. Nobody else fancies the trip.'

Whether it was Aunt Maud's constant criticism of his expectorating brown gobs of tobacco, or what, but about midday Biedler pulled his hat down over his brow and shouted:

'Me an' Jack are gonna scout on ahead. You'll be all right with Gary. We'll see you at the ranch.'

That was about three in the afternoon, before Gibbins had lost his rag and set the buggy going at suicidal speed. They had watched the burly sheriff and Jack put spurs to their mustangs and ride away until they were lost ahead in the distance.

'Any sign of Mr Biedler?' Heather asked Rusty as he carried in logs and knelt to light the pot-belly stove in the kitchen.

'Who, the sheriff? Nope. No sign of him. Only some other feller who called in, stopped awhile, an' said he was goin' on to the Topaz ranch. Brad, thass what he called himself.'

'Oh, that no-good,' Maud interposed. 'I'd like to know what he's up to. Causing mayhem somewhere without a doubt.'

'Aunt, please, he's not that bad.'

'So, why did he refuse to help us?'

'Perhaps he was in a hurry. I was surprised he didn't offer to show us the way, I must admit.'

'A selfish ruffian. We should have no more to do with him.'

Just then there was a commotion outside in the dark and, eventually, Biedler stomped in, carrying his rifle. It was a long-barrelled Remington rolling block, fitted with a telescope, chambered to take cartridges of .45-120 calibre: powerful kicking power. It had cost him 200 dollars so he never left it outside with his horse.

'Hello, Sheriff,' Heather greeted him. 'We thought you would have been here before now.'

'No, we made a detour to make sure there weren't none of them lariat Indians skulking around,' he replied, gruffly, warming his backside at the fire. 'All seems clear. You'll be quite safe tonight.'

'Why do they call them lariat Indians?'

'Because they generally have a lariat snaked over their shoulders. They use 'em to sneak up and steal hosses. They'll have 'em away right from under your nose.'

'Yeah,' Garry guffawed, scratching at himself, and giving Maud a nudge. 'They'd have your calico drawers off, darlin', 'fore you felt the draught.'

'How dare you!' Maud flicked at him with her fingers. 'Clear off, you smelly old man.'

'Aw, come, sweetheart.' The old-timer made a clucking noise and clutched at Maud's backside beneath her skirt. 'You might be a bony ol' broiler but surely ye got a bit of life left down below?'

Maud screeched her horror, staring at his wrinkled hairy chops. She bashed at him with her parasol. 'Get away from me.'

'Aw, ye know ye like it.Ye ain't such a withered ol' prune, really.'

'Get out. Go away. You can sleep in the stable. I

don't want you in my house. I've never been so insulted.'

'Keep waitin', missus,' Gibbins called as he hobbled arthritically out. 'I'll think up some more.'

As he stepped out through the front door he shouted: 'Waal, lookee who's here. If it ain't that tall, dark stranger ye've been on about. Howdy, Brad, where've ya been?'

'Howdy, Gary.' Bradshaw patted his shoulder and went into the ranch house. 'Sheriff, just the man I want. There's been another attempted killin' along at Mizpah Creek. Young Rodrigo's hurt bad. Might not live, and I was lucky to escape with my life.'

'That's your story, is it?' Maud asked. 'How do we know it wasn't you doing the shooting? I wouldn't be surprised.'

'Quit it, lady. I don't want another run-in with you.' Brad turned his attention to Biedler's rifle. 'Mind if I take a look at this?' He cocked an eye at the sheriff as he sniffed at the barrel. 'You been shooting this not so long ago?'

'Sure have. I got a buck hanging over the back of my saddle to prove it.' Biedler bridled up. 'Just what in hell are you tryin' to suggest?'

'A fine weapon. You could easily take a man out from half a mile with this.'

'Get lost. I don't like the tone of your voice. What you doing here, anyhow? You wanna watch that mouth of yourn, Bradshaw, or it could be you who gits arrested and strung up. We don't waste time in these parts.'

'No, so I've noticed.' Brad tossed the rifle back hard at him. 'Who else are you with?'

'Scarface Jack Mosby.'

'Where is he?'

'How the hell do I know. We split up to circle around on the look-out for Sioux. He'll be back soon.'

'In that case I'll want a word or two with him,' Bradshaw drawled. 'So what you gonna do about Rodrigo?'

'I'll look into it tomorrow. It's my guess it was one of his Mex *compadres* who he'd gypped at cards or who'd put his nose out of joint.'

'If so why did he want me dead, too? It's my opinion, Sheriff, that something fishy's going on in these parts.'

'You're entitled to your opinion. In the meantime, it's too dark to do anything about it now. We'll have supper and bed down here, Miss Monro.'

'Certainly, Sheriff, you're welcome to eat with us,' Heather said. 'It was very kind of you to see us safely to the ranch.'

'I'm not having *that* man eating with us.' Aunt Maud jabbed her parasol at Brad. 'He can join those other riff-raff in the bunkhouse. Tomorrow I want him off my premises.'

'*Your* premises?' Brad grinned, sardonically, as he adjusted his bullet-shattered Stetson. 'For an old buzzard you're pretty hot off the mark, aincha?'

'Really, Aunt,' Heather protested, 'I'd like Mr

Bradshaw to stay.'

'Don't worry about it, Heather. It might give me indigestion if I had to dine with her.'

But, as he stepped outside, Heather followed him.

'Brad,' she called out. 'What's going on? Have you discovered anything?'

'Not a lot that adds up 'cept that somebody don't want me around. Not only your aunt.' He pulled her back into shadows with him and caught hold of her slim waist. 'How about you?'

'Please,' she said, struggling against him. 'Not after what I saw in the livery barn yesterday.'

'Aw, that.' He grinned at her, a tad shamefaced. 'That weren't nuthin'. I was just trying to find out if she was an Amazon.'

'A what?'

'An Amazon. A warrior queen. That's what she fancies herself as. I heard tell they have one breast cut off. I was investigating.'

'Oh, you! You're not the decent man I thought you were. What are you, some sort of rough-riding Romeo?'

'I guess I should admit she ain't. An Amazon, I mean. She's got the regulation two. Aw, I was only trying to take her down a peg or two.'

'It looked to me like you were intent on doing more than that. No, please, don't.' She tried to prevent his big hands from sliding up towards her own anatomy. 'Where I come from, if a man does that he should expect to marry a girl.'

'How about if he kisses her?' Before she could stop him he was pulling her in tight and his lips were on hers. For seconds she succumbed to the embrace, but then she tried pushing him off, thumping at his chest with her fists.

'Leave me alone,' she gasped. 'Really!'

'You sound like your aunt.' Brad held on to her. 'Ain't I decent enough for you? Don't worry, honey, where I come from just 'cause a man kisses a gal it don't mean he's planning on gittin' hitched.'

There was a loud and ironic wolf-whistle. Looking around Brad saw Scarface Jack sitting on his bronco grinning.

'For a man who says he wouldn't work for wimmin you sure making a good shot at smoochin' up to the new ranch-owner lady,' he crowed. 'Go on, boy, don't let me stop you. Go on, get in there!'

'Good-night, Heather. Things will sort themselves out, I hope.' Brad pressed her hands and jumped down from the porch to follow Jack who was saun-tering away with his horse towards the corral. 'Hey, you,' he shouted. 'I got some questions to ask you.'

Heather watched him go and wondered if he would resort to fisticuffs or, worse, firearms, again. He was, she guessed, a very violent, amoral, danger-ous man. In fact, they *all* seemed to be those things out here. But somehow she felt he wouldn't get anything out of that scarfaced scallywag. So she sighed, touching her lips, remembering the brief kiss, and went back inside. Like he had said, saved by the bell! Another ten minutes outside under the stars and he might have swept her off her feet.

The girl had difficulty sleeping what with the shrill nasal vibrations of Maud's snoring, the scuttling of mice or rats, and the howling of wolves or coyotes out on the prairie. She tossed and turned, thinking of the tall, roughly handsome frontiersman. She had never met a man like him. It was as if she were attracted and repelled by him at one and the same time. Exhausted, she rose at the first glimmer of dawn and went outside. How lonesome this country was, so far from civilized society. The prairie stretched away into the distance like an endless ocean, the sky and clouds so vast she felt swamped by space.

Heather tried to pump water from the well, but it was a laborious task and one she was not accustomed to. What a hard life a woman would have out here! It would be, for sure, one long round from dawn 'til dusk of fetching water and fuel, feeding hens and hogs, washing clothes, mending, darning, giving birth, raising children, cooking over a primitive stove, on and on. No wonder many of these local women looked so drab and worn-out before thirty. And what was there to do if she had any spare time? There were no books, no museums, no paintings, no libraries, no magazines, no high fashion, no opera, no theatre, apart from that hut of a place in Miles City, no intelligent society, nothing, not even, it seemed, law and order, the nearest medical help forty miles away. The long winters would seem interminable. Even now, in this late spring, the incessant prairie wind had begun to grate on her nerves.

'Let's face it,' she whispered, 'I'm homesick for Boston. I'd never fit in out here.' Not unless she had a strong, rugged husband to help them carve out a decent life. Maybe then. . . .

Brad Bradshaw was on one knee, apparently deep in thought, beside two earth-mound graves, marked only by rugged wooden crosses, when she saw him. He rose and met her eyes. 'One day I'll get 'em a good stone memorial, maybe even black marble,' he drawled. He grinned at her. 'You're up early.'

'I couldn't sleep. I've been wondering what to do. My aunt plans to sell up this place, go back East. In one way I would like to try to make a go of it. It seems cowardly to give up and run away.'

'This country is no place for amateurs. It's rough, tough country. It's defeated many a man. And there ain't many wimmin run a ranch on their own. A few, but they're a special breed.'

'If we could find a good foreman. You wouldn't reconsider staying on to help us out?'

'What, work for that cantankerous old sourpuss? No way,' he drawled. 'I'd rather walk than ride for *her*. What you've got to do, Heather, is decide who's in charge between you two.'

'So, where are you going?'

'Over to the del Toro spread. I'm gonna offer my services to them.'

'But wouldn't you be working for a woman there? They say he's crippled and that crazy girl more or less runs the place.'

'That's what *she* thinks!' He had walked back with Heather to the corral and whistled to Blaze. He climbed over the rail and got hold of the horse with the easy assurance he did most things. He was a man who had been brought up in the West. Bridling and saddling a bronc was second nature to him. He hardly had to think about it. Heather bit her lip as she watched, pulling her shawl around her shoulders, the wind whipping her hair across her eyes. She herself had never even learned to ride. A bitter envy rose in her.

'I suppose you prefer that wildcat's company?' she cried. 'You're two of a kind.'

'Hey,' he called, swinging aboard Blaze, his Winchester slung today across his back. 'Don't get het up. To tell you the truth I ain't got much time. If I get in there with 'em it seems to me I'll be better positioned to find out what's going on.'

'Aren't you going to wait for the sheriff?'

'What'n hell use is he?' he called, as he circled the sprightly chestnut away. '*Adios*, gal, I'll be seein' you.'

Heather watched him go, riding straight-backed, tall in the saddle, and bit her lip with irritation. Oh,

God! she thought. I practically threw myself at him. And all I got for my trouble was a kick in the teeth. What a fool I am! Perhaps Aunt Maud is right. We ought to go home.

SEVEN

The sun was rising high, steaming out the winter damp as a detachment of the Seventh Cavalry wheeled out of Fort Keogh, two miles from Miles City, and set off at a cracking pace along the bank of the Yellowstone River. In the lead was Captain George Hetherington, accompanied by the 'shave-tail' lieutenant, Claud Page, and their standard-bearer holding aloft the stars and bars to ripple proudly in the strong breeze as they rode.

It was Page's first taste of a real scouting expedition and his face was flushed with excitement. 'Do you think we'll come across any renegades, Captain?' he called out.

'Who knows? Red Panther ain't hampered by having any squaws, children, dogs or village baggage with him. He and his warriors ride free and fast. So we don't really have much clue where he'll be, eh, Mr Kelly?'

He addressed the remark to the quiet American

who rode a few paces behind. The company's chief scout, Luther Kelly, was in civilian clothes: a broad-brimmed hat, buckskin jacket over roll-neck jersey and riding britches, clean-shaven but for a moustache.

'True,' he muttered. 'Your guess is as good as mine, Cap'.'

Known as 'Yellowstone', or 'Kelly the Sphinx' by the soldiers at Fort Keogh, the scout was a descendant of Hannah Dustin, a New England woman who had been captured by Indians during the war with the French and had made a remarkable escape. A well-educated, quiet-spoken man, he was a lover of the wild and more familiar than most with this terrain.

'It might interest you to know, Page, that we're following the same route as Custer on his fatal last ride,' Captain Hetherington pointed out.

'I hope you ain't planning on going at his pace,' Kelly called. 'He wore his men and horses to a frazzle.'

'We may have to if we're to catch him. There's a message come through that Red Panther and his boys were seen passing the St Labre mission and heading up Otter Creek.'

'Did they attack the mission, sir?' Lieutenant Page asked.

'No. They regard the Black Robes as a tad crazy and give 'em a wide berth. Father Jean and his nuns have never had much luck converting them from their heathen ways. You could count on the fingers of one hand those they've brought into the fold. The Sioux aren't inclined to give up their gods. Nor their bigamy, or trigamy, you might say. But they seem to respect Father Jean's "magic" and leave him in peace.'

'A pity they don't feel the same way about the other settlers,' Kelly drawled as he rode. 'Red Panther is one of the most murderous Indians I've ever come across. Treacherous, too. A burning ranch and mutilated corpses are his signature and all he usually leaves in his wake.'

It was easy enough to converse. They rode at a steady lope, for the Yellowstone valley was broad, the embankment of the river level and smooth, almost a bridle path for the cavalry. They had yet to encounter rougher terrain.

'I know I'm new out here, sir,' Page said, 'but wouldn't it make more sense to go up the Tongue River? It seems to be the direct route to the mission.'

'You don't catch Indians by going straight after them, lieutenant. You have to try to catch them in a net. We'll camp at the mouth of Rosebud Creek tonight, then head across to Fort Custer on the Big Horn. That way we might cut across their trail.'

Claud Page felt like replying that it seemed a waste of time to him, but he guessed that these old hands knew best. He fell silent, like the others. They needed to save their breath and energy for the long ride ahead. Each man was carrying forty rounds of ammunition and hard-tack rations to last five days. After that they would have to live off the land. The prospect of possible action or battle excited the young officer. What a tale he would have to tell Heather Monro if they met again!

Meanwhile, as he rode up Mizpah Creek, Brad noticed a narrow coulée leading off to the west. He thought he heard the lowing of cattle coming from it, so he nosed Blaze quietly through. Its steep, pine-girt sides, still patched with snow, gave way to a grassy valley where at least 300 head of cattle were grazing, bulls, cows and calves. In attendance were two *cibeleros*, Mexicans who carried long lances with which they controlled the herd. Brilliant horsemen, they scorned to use rifles to kill buffalo and would race along beside a fleeing bull like the Sioux to bring him down with their lance.

Brad pulled Blaze in behind a large rock and found a small brass telescope in his warbag. He extended it and took a peep, sweeping it from one beast to the other.

'Well, whadda ya know?' he whispered. 'The Diamond Square brand. Looks like little Miss del Toro has been helping herself to Rob's cattle.'

He began to remove his Winchester from his back, an anger seething in him, ready to take a pop shot at the two *cibeleros*, but what would be the good of that? It would only stampede the herd. He left them and quietly returned to the Mizpah stream, going on his way deep in thought.

There was an armed guard on the gate of the del Toros' small fortress, who began clanging a bell as he saw the stranger approach.

'Wha' you wan', greengo?' He peered from his bell-tower along the sights of his rifle at Bradshaw.

'Open up,' Brad shouted, sitting his horse. 'I wanna see your boss.'

Euala de Toro had stepped out on to the veranda of the ranch house when she heard the bell tolling. Slim and shapely in her tight-fitting Spanish blouse and her *chaparreras*, the prairie wind blowing her mass of jet black hair across her face, she stood, boots firmly planted, a carbine held aimed at the rider. She levered a slug into the breech as he drew near.

'That's close enough. Take that revolver from your holster nice an' slow and toss it over here.'

'What you scared of?' Brad asked. 'You figure I've come about stolen cattle?'

'What stolen cattle?'

'The ones you've got cooped up in that coulée guarded by your men. Don't play the innocent. They've got the Diamond Square brand on 'em. I might remind you there's swift justice in Montana for cattle-thieves. Nobody would blame me if I killed you on the spot.'

'You could try.' Euala tossed her hair back, angrily, and nodded at two of her *charros* who sat their mustangs on either side, guns covering him. 'But it would be you who would die. So you had better do as

91

I say. Throw your revolver down. I have heard you are fast but you are not fast enough for three of us.'

Brad gave a rueful grin and touched the scab on his earlobe where her bullet had nicked it the day before.

'You're pretty fast yourself. Tell me, were you aiming for this or my heart?'

'You're a fool. You come here insulting us. We ought to kill you.'

'Whadda ya mean, insulting you? You claiming you ain't a thief like your brother?'

Euala jagged her lips back in an angry grimace.

'I put those beeves there for their own safety so that whoever takes over the Diamond Square will have the nucleus of a herd to start themselves off with. The rest have been run off.'

'Who by?'

'How do I know? Rustlers.'

'But they ain't taken none of yourn?'

'We guard ours well.'

'I betcha do. Waal,' he drawled, 'I guess I'm gonna have to give you the benefit of the doubt. But I ain't giving up my Remington. Not to no woman.'

Euala fired the carbine from the hip without warning. Blaze whinnied and jumped as the bullet whistled past Brad's other ear. He tensed on the reins and scowled at her.

'Nearly.' Her lips curled back over her white teeth in a mocking smile. 'No, I wasn't aiming for a heart shot. Now do you believe me?'

92

'Let's stop foolin' about, shall we, gal, or you might git me mad again. You got the advantage 'cause I don't aim to get myself a reputation for killin' a woman. Anyhow, you're too delectable a piece of feminine flesh to waste.'

'Delectable a piece . . .' She gave a scoffing laugh. 'Who do you think you *are*?'

'What's going on?' a gruff voice called in Spanish, as Antonio del Toro was pushed through the doorway in his wheelchair by one of his men.

'Just paying a social call, *señor*. But your daughter don't seem to appreciate it. I was wondering how your son is?'

Antonio's dark eyes clouded in a worried manner.

'He is not good. The bullet is still in his chest. We have sent Raoul to Fort Keogh to see if we can get medical aid. You must be the man called Bradshaw. I have heard of you. My daughter seems to be quite impressed by you.'

'Don't be stupid, Father.' Euala del Toro flared up, tossing her head like an angry horse. But blood was reddening the temples of her otherwise pale face in a giveaway sign. 'Why should I be impressed by this saddle tramp?'

'Step down, Mr Bradshaw, and come inside. You must be thirsty after your long ride.'

Brad swung lightly from the saddle, giving Blaze's reins to a Mexican boy groom. He patted the walnut grip of the Remington and jumped up the steps to the veranda, putting out a hand to gently push

Euala's carbine aside.

'Little gals didn't oughta play with guns,' he said. 'It's dangerous.'

'Hah!' She spat out words of Spanish that he could only assume registered her disgust, and followed him indoors. 'What are you really doing here?'

Brad doffed his gunshot Stetson and glanced around the spacious living-room which was comfortably decorated in the Spanish style.

'That was a twenty-dollar J.B. But I guess I got off light. How about if I take a look at your brother?'

The girl shrugged, led him to a back bedroom and indicated her brother lying in a cot.

'He has gone into a deep coma. We think it is too dangerous for us to probe for the bullet. It is not far from the heart.'

Brad studied the handsome youth, his silky black hair damp across his perspiring brow, and pulled down the sheet. His chest was heavily bandaged, and there was a nasty bloodstain. He lifted the bandage slightly and took a peek.

'Yeah, maybe you're right. But he's got the benefit of youth. Maybe he'll hang on.'

'My father will be devastated if he dies,' she said, in a whisper, 'even though he was disapointed in him. So will I.'

'He ain't dead yet.' Brad reached out and gripped her hand. 'His breathing's steady. I've seen worse.'

Euala pulled her arm away.

'I don't need your false sympathy. You hate us.

They all hate us.'

'Not all of us. Don't tar us all with the same racist brush.' He turned and went back to the main room where a chubby serving-woman was bringing in a tray loaded with sweetmeats and glasses of apple-juice.

'Seat yourself.' Antonio waved a hand towards a hide armchair. 'Is this drink OK or you want something stronger?'

'It's fine.' Brad took a glass and swigged half of its contents in one swallow. '*Muchas gracias*, ain't that what you say? Very thirst-quenching.'

'So, what brings you to these parts, *señor*?'

'I've come to ask for a job. Thought maybe you could do with another hand.'

'A job?' Euala sneered. 'What are you talking about?'

'A job, you know, paid work tending the herd or protecting it from these rustlers you talk about.'

'We could do with another gun,' Antonio said. 'I have the feeling you are an honest man even though you are a gringo. What sort of money are you looking for?'

'Regular wage, same as your other men. Say thirty a month all found.'

'Don't trust him,' Euala snapped. 'He is up to some trick. I don't want him here.'

'Don't you ever put a dress on?' Brad asked. 'You know, it would be nice to see you behave like a real woman. I've an idea you could be quite sweet.'

'You like my daughter, Brad? She is fiery, eh? Like I was when I was young.'

'Sure do. Why ride a mustang when you can have a thoroughbred? All she needs is a little schoolin'. Can she cook?'

'Are you talking about me?' Euala demanded. 'No, I don't cook. Cooking is for cooks. Washing clothes is for washerwomen. If you want a little tame wife you had better go back to that simpering gringo goody-goody who has been making eyes at you. I hear she is taking over the Diamond Square.'

'Not just yet, she ain't. But I'd rather you didn't speak about my friend like that. She's a nice gal. She don't go struttin' around shootin' people's ears off.'

'Ha! So you *do* like her!' Euala had seated herself on another chair, one booted leg crooked over her knee. She pointed an accusing finger at him. 'I don't wash and cook. Now my father is incapacitated I run this ranch. Any man don't do as I say, God help him. If you work here, be warned, gringo, I will ride you hard.'

'The harder the better.' Bradshaw gave her a lecherous grin, his grey eyes twinkling in their slits. 'That sounds fun.'

'Ah, you!' Euala jumped up and strode to the door. 'If you're working for us you can get out of here and go relieve the men guarding the Diamond Square herd. You won't be frightened to be alone at night?'

'Maybe you'd like to come and keep me company.'

'So, what are you waiting for?' She ignored his remark. 'On your horse, *hombre*.'

'You don't mind if I finish my refreshments first?' Brad waved her away with one hand. 'I was going to have a chat with your father. Oh, and by the way, I ain't planning on gittin' hitched so you needn't bother prettifying yourself up, after all.'

'Oh!' Euala, lost for words, walked out, slamming the door.

Her father laughed. 'Many a man has made that boast. Yet, some wild stallions who think they can roam free are roped and branded before they know it.'

'Not me. I ain't the marryin' kind.' The frontiersman stuffed a couple of spicy sweetmeats into his mouth and tucked some sugared biscuits into his shirt pocket for later consumption. 'No,' he said, swallowing a mouthful, 'I'm only joshing her.'

'You seem to get her steamed up, I notice,' Antonio remarked, wincing from the pain in his useless legs. 'As for my son, if you can bring me the man who shot him I will pay you handsomely.'

'No need to pay me. It would be a pleasure to catch him. He was aiming at me, too. Well, I guess I'd better get along to the coulée and get about my duties.'

'Will you be OK on your own? I can spare you another man if you wish, but we need to tend our own herd.'

'I like working alone,' Brad growled, getting to his feet. 'I feel safer.'

EIGHT

There was another visitor to the Diamond Square ranch: lawyer Charles Horniblow, riding in on horse-back. In his striped suit, which hugged his muscular physique, clean linen, loose bow, and velvet-collared topcoat, he bustled into the ranch house with the air of a man to whom time was money.

'So,' he called, in his husky voice, removing his curly-brimmed hat, 'have you decided to sell, or not?'

'Yes, we definitely have,' Aunt Maud replied. 'You colonists are welcome to these wild territories. Personally, I find the lax morals, the violent nature of the population, quite appalling.'

'In that case I'll make you an offer. I've a cheque here for a thousand dollars cashable at any Wells Fargo office for the land, buildings and stock, what's left of it. You won't get a better offer.'

'I don't know, Maud,' Heather shyly demurred. 'Surely the property is worth more than that and will be enhanced with time. A whole ranch this size for a thousand. It hardly seems enough.'

'I'll take it, 'Maud snapped. 'You have no say in the

98

matter.' As Horniblow took the banker's draft from
his inside pocket she quickly snatched it from him
and stuffed it into her handbag. 'Thank you, sir.
Presumably you have brought the agreement for me
to sign?'

'Sure have, ma'am. You're the gal's legal guardian
so you're the one we deal with. Where did I put it?
Ah, yes.' He pulled a document from his topcoat
pocket and proceeded to read out the specifications
of the property followed by what to his listeners
sounded like legal flapdoodle full of Latin phrases.
'That covers all eventualities. A copy for you and the
original for me.'

When Aunt Maud had appended her signature,
Heather suggested she ought to sign, too. 'No need
for that,' Horniblow said, waving the ink dry. 'So, now
I am the new owner of this ranch I assume you will be
leaving to catch the first steamer back downriver?'

'I certainly am. Heather, call that dreadful hirsute
person, what's his name, Gibbins, to come and pick
up my bags.'

'I . . . I'm not sure I agree with this,' Heather said,
with some hesitation. 'It all seems rather precipitate.
I would like to wait and see what Mr Bradshaw deems
best. Or, at least, say goodbye.'

'Too late. The business is transacted,' Maud
replied, briskly, attending to wrapping herself in coat
and muffler. 'But you wait, if you want to. I'll be off.
You can find me at the hotel in Miles City when
you're ready.'

Aunt Maud seemed extremely eager to be away, the cheque tucked in her pocket. 'Come along, man! Hurry up! Careful with those bags. Is the carriage ready?'

'Sure, it awaits your highness,' Gary Gibbins smirked. 'Nobody could be in a bigger hurry than me to see the back of you.'

'You're welcome to stay as long as you like, Miss Monro,' Horniblow told Heather, with a wide smile. 'If you want to see Bradshaw for a tender farewell I'll be glad to send for him. How does a rough hooligan like that manage to bowl all you gals off their feet? Even my bespectacled secretary's sighing about him.'

Heather could not help a blush rising to her cheeks.

'It's not like that,' she whispered. 'But that's very kind of you.'

Maud didn't even bother saying goodbye. She was hurrying out, clambering up on to the buckboard's seat.

'Get a move on, driver. We haven't got all day.'

'Keep your hair on, gal,' Gary shouted, climbing aboard, gathering the reins and shouting to the horses to get moving. 'I ain't nevuh come across a body like you. You got ants in your pants, or somethang?'

'Don't be insolent,' Maud replied, as they went rattling away.

'What I don't git is why the young gal ain't comin'

with us. Not that I blame her. What's your dad-blamed hurry?'

'If you really want to know, I am sick and tired of attending to that little hussy. If she wants to stay, so be it. She's set her cap at that uncouth, violent Bradshaw man. So, she's welcome to him. I can tell you, I'm catching the first steamboat back to civilization.'

'That ain't very nice, is it? You cain't jest walk out on the poor li'l bitch.'

'Can't I?' Maud cried, gleefully, pulling the cheque from her pocket and waving it. 'Once I cash this you won't see me for dust.' Gary Gibbins pondered on this as he drove the rig along the Powder and turned up the rough trail across the ridge towards Miles City, forty miles away.

'You know, that don't sound neither nice, nor legal to me.'

'Oh, fiddlesticks!' Maud screeched. 'At my age a spinster has to think of her own future. I've scrimped and sewed, wasted my younger days tending that family, the Monros. And for what? I know that girl wants to get rid of me, but is too frightened to say so. I've become a burden to her. Do you think that as soon as she gets married her dumbfool husband will want to take me as part of the package!'

'No, I sure as tarnation wouldn't think so. You got a point there, gal. What, a miserable old boot like you? No way.'

Maud frowned at him, but brandished the cheque again.

'A thousand. Paid to me in my name. This is my nest-egg. And I intend to make sure it's all mine.' She added, plaintively: 'What else could I do? What would happen to a poor, destitute lady of my years? Who would want me? Where would I go?'

'Thar, thar, gal.' Gary put an arm around her and gave her a hug. 'Don't take on so. I guess the filly can take care of herself. In a way, I don't blame you. Out here it's dog eat dog. What'll happen to a poor fella like me when I cain't work no more? I'll be in the gutter, that's what.'

'Well,' Maud primly removed his arm, 'you won't find me there with you.'

Back at the ranch Horniblow beckoned Scarface Jack to join him outside.

'Get on your pinto and go after Gibbins and that old dame. Make sure they don't reach Miles City. I don't want her cashing that cheque. I'll take care of the girl. Might have a bit of fun with her before I give her the chop. We can blame it on the Indians.'

'Hey, how come you git all the best jobs? I'd like to take a poke at that bit of muslin, too.'

'Because I'm the boss. I'll see you OK, Jack. Just do as I say. We don't want no comeback.'

'Seems a pity to waste a purty li'l bit of fluff like that. But I guess it has to be.' Jack went to jump on his horse, dragging its head around and calling out: 'It'll be a pleasure to take care of Gibbins, the noisy old fool, and that ol' shrew. See ya, boss.'

Horniblow watched him go, glanced into the house where Heather Monro was busy washing plates in the kitchen, and went to roust up the hands. Rusty and the other boys were leaning on the corral fence awaiting orders.

'Right, fellas,' the lawyer shouted, beaming proudly, 'I'm the new owner of the Diamond Square. Funny, ain't it? What's the matter, Murphy, you're not laughing? Well, I'll be wanting to see some work done from here on. No more sitting on your butts. To start with I want every single cow rounded up, them that's left, ready for beef-shipping time. So, on your broncs, boys, and out on the range. OK?'

Lonesome Bradshaw didn't feel easy as darkness closed in that night. The coulée was longer and wider than he had thought it to be. He sent the two *cibeleros* back to the Topaz ranch and made camp at the far end where it seemed entry could be made down a steep slope, or cattle could be driven up out.

'I gotta keep an eye on the back door,' he called to Blaze who was munching at the fresh grass, his saddle loose-cinched. Brad occupied himself cutting pine boughs with his razor-sharp Bowie and erecting a lean-to. Then he settled down by his fire and waited for the coffee-pot to boil and bubble.

Before the moon began its rise from behind the cliffs it became pitch dark. Any man would have found it pretty eerie listening to the shrill calls of night predators. Or might they be Indians on the prowl? There was a *whoosh* of wingbeats and a huge owl, white and ghostly, swooped through the branches past his head, and there was a screech of terror as it pounced on a jack rabbit.

'I'm too easy a target sittin' here,' Brad muttered. He picked up his Spencer carbine and prowled away to take up position crouched between the roots of a big birch. The night was chill and he jerked up the collar of his worn navy-blue topcoat. All he had to do now was try not to go to sleep. But he'd been in the saddle all day and . . .

Suddenly, there was the swish of parting air as a lance hissed towards him and nearly parted his own hair. It thudded into the bole of the birch, its shaft twanging. Maybe he had dozed off for the edge of the moon was creeping up behind a jagged peak, casting wavering shadows through the trees and across the silver-streaked pasture.

Brad ducked down, instinctively, and froze, trying to peer through the half-light. There was no sound. The shaft of the lance had no feathers or scalps hanging from it. More like a *cibelero*'s. Brad put his Spencer aside drew his Bowie, and slithered off on all fours, propelling himself with knees and elbows, slowly, silently, through the undergrowth, in a semi-circle towards where the lance had been thrown. He paused, listening, heard the crack of a twig and, eventually, the rasp of breath as a man crept through the low branches towards him.

The frontiersman froze as a dark figure loomed

up, a man in black. He, too, had a knife in his grip. Brad waited until he was almost on him, then caught his ankle with his free hand and with his right elbow on the knee forced his attacker to fall back.

Then he made a catlike leap to land upon him, grabbed the wrist of his knife-hand and jabbed the point of his Bowie into his throat. The point pricked blood and, although his instinct was to plunge it further, he held back.

'Hold it, you snake. Come creeping up on me in the dark, would ye?' He stared into the tense face of Raoul Vasconcelos. 'Drop that knife 'less you want your gizzard slit.'

When Raoul did as he was bid, Brad hauled him over on his face, then to his feet, keeping a hand in his hair and the knife to his throat. He frog-marched him back to the fire, reached for his lariat from his saddle horn, forced the Mexican to his knees and fisted him hard across the back of his neck. While he was stunned he swiftly bound his ankles and wrists behind him, noosing the rawhide rope tight around his throat and giving it a vicious jerk. When he was hogtied he pushed him over on his back.

'So, what's this all about? he growled. 'What's your interest in sneaking up, trying to kill me?'

Raoul stared at him, his dark eyes blazing with hatred.

'Yes, I try to kill you. You come here trying to take her away from me. You are no good to her. You can

105

only make her unhappy.'

'Who? Oh, her. The fast-shootin' filly. You want to kill me out of jealousy? You sure got it bad, pal.'

'What you wan' here? Why don' you go back to the gringo girl?'

'Hell,' Brad growled. 'You're a weird one.'

But his ears pricked up as he suddenly heard men's voices drifting on the night breeze, the whinnying of horses, and the rumble of cattle on the move. 'Shee-it! They're down the far end. They're taking the cattle. Are they with you?'

Raoul shook his head. 'No. Untie me. You need my help.'

'Like I need a hole in the head. No thanks. I can do without you riding behind me.'

Brad pulled the lance from the tree, tightened the cinch of Blaze's saddle, unhitched him, slung the Spencer to hang from the saddle horn and himself on to the back as he sent the chestnut careering away, easing his boots into the bentwood stirrups as he rode.

There were five of them, men bundled up in macinaws and hats, cracking lariat ends as whips, driving the restless herd of seething, horn-tossing cattle before them out of the coulée.

'Hold it!' he yelled as he caught up with the *hombre* riding drag. It might seem quixotic but his instinct was to give a man a chance, not to hit him in the back.

The man turned, but it was too dark to see his

face, and he was dragging out a big old cap-and-ball revolver from his belt. He swung it on Bradshaw and there was a flash of flame as he fired. Brad hurled the lance and it went through the man's chest, catapulting him from his bronc. The explosion set the bulls, cows and calf longhorns racing away as if at the sound of a starter's gun. The rider on point screamed as the seething mass of hide and horn engulfed him and he was thrown from his pony, tossed in the air like a rag-doll by a set of vicious horns and trampled underneath as the stampede pounded over him.

The other three rustlers set off, screaming and slashing their ropes, trying to head off the beasts as they charged alongside, but it was too late; they were streaming out of the coulée on to the plain. There would be no stopping them now for ten miles or more.

The men, too, wanted to know what the shooting was about. Brad had jumped from his horse and gone down on one knee, peering at the face of the man on his back with the lance in his chest. It was Danny Murphy. He was dead.

Brad pulled Blaze back to him, unhooked the Spencer, cast the horse away, and went down on one knee again as the rustlers rode back up the slope towards him, a threat in the manner of their approach.

'Throw your guns down, boys,' he shouted, hauling Murphy up to hold as a shield before him. 'Ain't one dead enough?'

The first rider fired his handgun and blood spurted from Murphy's chest, splashing over the Kansan. Brad laid the Spencer aside and reached for his Remington now that they were within range. Holding Murphy aloft with his left grip, he held the six-gun with outstretched arm. His first bullet caught the cowboy in the abdomen. He doubled up and rolled from his mustang to the ground.

'That's two down,' he shouted. 'Who's gonna be next?'

Curses came from the snarling lips of the two men as they spurred their mustangs towards him, sending slugs of lead whining past his head. Murphy caught another in the chest as Brad gritted his teeth and returned fire, loosing off every bullet in his cylinder, finally making good, piercing the jugular of a bearded rider, who hit the ground and rolled away to lie on his side, gouting blood.

The last man was almost upon him, gunfire flashing as he charged, and Brad hurled the empty Remington at him. The heavy steel weapon scored a lucky hit to his jaw, making him throw up his gun hand.

Brad snatched up the Spencer, jumped to his feet, and gave him a mighty crack across the chest as he passed, swinging the carbine like a club.

'Jeez!' he grinned in triumph, 'I oughta play for the Dodgers.'

The cowboy had kicked up his heels and landed

on the ground hard. Brad pounced on him, twisted his revolver from his grip and gasped as he tore his bandanna mask away.

'Rusty! Well, I'll be damned. It was you guys stealing from Rob.'

The crack of a rifle shot and a bullet whistling past his head made him spin around. A rider on a black stallion was coming fast at him, a rifle gripped at shoulder-height, firing as he approached. Brad glimpsed tossing black hair. *She*, to be precise.

'It's me,' he shouted. 'Quit firing, you fool.'

Euala del Toro galloped her stallion up to him and drew up in a slither of turf as the steed's sharp hoofs carved up sods.

'I thought you were one of them,' she shouted, her teeth glistening in a taunting smile. 'Sorry.'

'Yeah, I'm sure you did.'

'Did I give you a fright?' She laughed as she jumped down and took a look at Murphy and the other bodies. 'You certainly haven't been wasting your time.'

'Four dead, although you won't find much left of the one riding point. Churned up into chicken soup, is my guess. And your charming lover is back at my camp trussed up. He tried to slice off my head with that lance.'

'Raoul? Why? He's no lover of mine.'

'He seems to be enamoured enough of you to kill. God knows why! I'd rather share my bed with a rattlesnake.'

109

'I wasn't trying to kill you. I couldn't see who you were in the dark.' She glanced at Brad and went over to gaze at Rusty, who was groaning as he regained his senses. 'This one works at the Diamond Square.'

'Yeah, funny, ain't it?' He got down on one knee beside the young puncher. 'Who's behind you boys. Who you selling the cattle to? Come on, you better talk.'

'Nobody,' Rusty protested. 'We're not bandits. We came up here to get the cattle back for the Diamond Square. Horniblow told us to. He's the new owner. We didn't know you were here and would start shooting. Christ, is that Murphy? Where are the others.'

'All dead.'

'Dead? Why? We weren't doing anything wrong.'

Brad cuffed him, viciously, across the jaw.

'You're lying. You heard me call out. I gave you a chance to surrender. You musta known it was me. But you came in shooting. I didn't wanna kill your pals but they forced my hand. You all tried to kill me. So unless I start getting some straight answers I'm mad enough to send you to join 'em. What's going on? Speak up, sunshine, and you ride out of here a free man. If not—'

'Hit me all you like.' Rusty raised his arm to protect himself as the tall Kansan raised his fist again. 'I don't care. I'm telling you the truth. You can hand me over to the sheriff. He'll clear me. We were doing nothing wrong.'

'Yeah? A friend of yourn, is he?'

'They ride like thieves in the night,' the girl cried as several of her *vaqueros* arrived to join them. 'Leave him to us. We will make him talk. How will he like having his hands crushed beneath a wagon wheel? He would never shoot a gun again.'

'Yeah, waal . . .' Brad drawled, holding her back. 'You're a bloodthirsty li'l gofer, aincha? Maybe, legally, him and t'others *thought* they were working for the owner of those longhorns. By the way, didn't we oughta git after 'em?'

'My men have slowed the herd down. It will stop when it reaches the Powder. The Diamond Square can have them back.'

'Huccome you were riding this way?'

'You know,' she remarked, with a bright smile, 'I had a hunch you might run into trouble. I still don't believe this guy. He's hiding someone. Maybe we should hang him high? That's range justice for cattle-thieves, as you yourself said.'

'Don't let her, Mr Bradshaw,' Rusty stuttered. 'Keep her away from me.'

'Yeah, you better go pick up your boyfriend, Raoul.' Brad put hands on her shoulders and turned her around. 'I'm taking this one back to the Diamond Square.'

'*Sí*, so you can look a hero in front of the pretty white *muchacha*?' Euala threw his arms off. 'You lousy peeg.'

'Calm down. What gets into you Mexicans? You be a good gal and go on home. I got things to do.' He waggled the Remington at Rusty, then holstered it. 'Get on your hoss, cowboy. If you try any funny tricks they'll be your last. I'll be riding behind you.'

He slung the Spencer over his back and vaulted into the saddle.

'Hyah!' he shouted, riding away back down the coulée. 'Let's go.'

'*Basta!*' The girl watched him go. 'Come back. You work for me now.' Her shouted words echoed along the valley. 'You dirty gringo. You're all alike. You theenk you so clever. You stay with her, I keel you.'

Brad looked back and waved heedlessly, before loping his horse away back towards the Diamond Square ranch.

NINE

The Minneconjou medicine-man, Wraps-Up-His-Tail, had an amazing secret. He was invulnerable to bullets. He could decapitate whites by pointing his captured cavalry sword at them. He could paint his face by merely pointing his finger at the sun. And he could cut down pines by making a sweeping motion of the sword. Although few Indians had actually witnessed this, except perhaps when in a fast or whiskey-trance, he was implicitly believed. The Minneconjou needed a small miracle if they were ever to win back their land of the buffalo from the white man. So, a small but fanatical band of warriors had been inflamed, about twenty braves in all, and rode out of the reservation to join him and the battle-scarred warrior, Red Panther.

Since the Custer massacre, in which he had played a leading role, Red Panther had carried on a bitter lone war against the conquerors of his people, the army, the cattlemen, and the filthy tribe of itinerant

113

hunters who had moved in to exterminate the bison of the northern plains. In the past decades they had slaughtered those of the southern prairies, to deprive nomadic red people of the very staple of life.

Red Panther's secret was to 'fly light', travel fast, make lightning strikes, killing cattle, stealing horses, hitting lone ranches, bull trains, stagecoaches, army paymasters' wagons or small patrols, hitting them hard and with a vengeance, and riding on.

Like their medicine man's marvellous powers, it was as if Red Panther's spirit guide made him invisible, directed his pony's feet, guided him as he and his band rode from the Powder westward to Otter Creek, on to Wolf Mountain to get the lie of the land and look out for pursuit, or to double back down the Rosebud where Red Panther had distinguished himself by his ferocity in another big battle, stopping General Crook and his column in their tracks. Or he would lead his warriors across the plains to the Greasy Grass stream where a pile of bones whitened by the wind was all that remained of Yellow Hair and his men.

Recently, after wintering in the caves of the towering Big Horn mountains, the warriors had descended to the plains again to attack a double wagon drawn by twenty mules proceeding up the reopened Bozeman Trail. They had killed the driver and found to their joy that the cargo was cases of fine Sharps rifles and ammunition headed for Fort Custer. There were also casks of whiskey so the warriors had had a fine old time.

Each warrior had taken a carbine. They had hidden a cache of others and burned or destroyed what they could not carry. Then they had set off back east across the plains looking for further prey as summer dawned. Now they were camped in Lame Deer Creek, an offshoot of the Rosebud, beneath Wolf Mountain.

Red Panther was a handsome man, his thick black hair swept high over his brow to hang loose around the crimson wool shirt that was his trademark. He wore leggings, moccasins, but scorned much decoration, just a high-collared necklace of bear's teeth, an animal he had slain in close-hand combat, and large golden loops in his ears.

He was seated around the fire with his trusted leaders, Deaf Bull, Sees-With-Ears, Cold Hail, Knows-His-Coups, Crazy Head, and, of course, Wraps-Up-His-Tail. Others of the band were busy cooking supper, the ribs of a longhorn they had killed, swinging them back and forth on a rope across the hot embers.

'My *Wyakin* tells me we must head for Moon Creek,' Red Panther grunted. 'The horse-soldiers have gone off on a fool's ride. Now is our chance to raid along the Yellow River.' His men nodded in agreement. Few cared to argue with the ferocious Red Panther. He had the power. And he was rarely wrong.

*

'Hi!' Scarface Jack called as he spurred his mustang to catch up with Gary Gibbins and Maud as they travelled across the prairie. 'Mr Horniblow sent me along. He figured you oughta have some protection with Red Panther on the prowl.'

'Aw, we don't need you, you rattlesnake,' Gibbins growled. 'You an' your kind's more trouble than the pesky Injins.'

Jack Mosby guffawed in his loose-lipped way.

'Listen to the old-timer.' He jogged along beside them, nonetheless. 'Cheer up, folks. Summer's on its way. Listen to all them frogs a'croakin'. Look at how the grass is greening an' all them purty flowers flowering' – ain't they yeller daisies? An' what's them other thangs?'

'The mauve ones are hyacinths and the white ones Mariposa lilies,' Maud replied in her teacherly manner, pointing with her parasol. 'That carmine colour is just common vetch, but I must admit it's quite pleasant out here when the sun shines.'

'Comin' in to all that cash seems to have put a shine on the old boot,' Mosby said, with a sneering grin. 'She's suddenly changed her tune.'

'Heck, she ain't so bad.' Gary gave Maud's bony knee a squeeze, making her squeal. 'Not when you git to know her. Hey, missus, mebbe when you cash that cheque you an' me kin go out an' celebrate?'

'Perish the thought,' Maud snapped. 'That is my nest-egg. I don't intend frittering it away, certainly not on drunken old fools like you.'

Mosby could have killed them both there and then. But why should Horniblow have it all his own way? 'He owes me,' he muttered. 'Does he think I'm stupid, doing his dirty work for him?' He would wait until the old hen cashed the cheque. That way nobody would suspect him. Then he would find some quiet alley to relieve her of the spondulicks.

However, the bank was closed by the time they reached Miles City late in the evening.

'What a nuisance,' Maud cried, clambering down. 'I'll have to book into the hotel overnight. I won't be needing my trunk. You can take it down to the water-front. I'll be taking the first steamship out in the morning.'

'Anything your ladyship says,' Gary responded, testing the silver dollar she gave him for the ride between his false teeth. 'You sure you can spare this?'

Scarface Jack naturally gravitated towards a tour of the saloons and parlour houses. There was no sign of Sam Rollins in the Steamboat. 'Where's he got to?' he demanded of the freckle-faced boy who was trying to cope behind the bar.

'He's gone out to the Diamond Square ranch,' the boy piped up. 'He said something about a show-down.'

'A showdown? What's he on about? Maybe they're planning to dispose of that tall stranger, Bradshaw? Not before time. He sure likes sticking his nose in. Sam musta taken a different trail to us. Gimme a bottle of the best red-eye, son. Might as well spend what I got left. I'll be in the money tomorrow.'

'How's that?' the boy asked, as he filled a bottle from a cask below the bar.

Jack tapped his nose and winked.

'Ask no questions an' you git told no lies. But I can tell you, boy, I'll be bidding farewell to Miles City.'

Yeah, he thought, as he pulled a swallow from the upheld bottle, three swallows, in fact, and gave a gasp of satisfaction. I'll have to git outa this town 'fore Horniblow comes lookin' for me.

Just then Captain Grant Marsh ambled into the Steamboat and stood at the bar.

'Howdy, Cap',' Jack called, going to stand beside him. He poured a tumbler full of cornjuice for the uniformed steamboat man. 'How's tricks? Where's your next trip?'

Normally Marsh would have avoided the company of a river rat like Mosby, but he knew he had an explosive temper and psychopathic tendencies, so he accepted the drink.

'I'm going on up river in the morning as far as the mouth of the Big Horn,' he mumbled through his beard. 'I got military supplies to deliver to Fort Custer.'

'You don't say.' Jack leered at him, leaning on the bar, slurping from the bottle. 'You can take that big boat all that way?'

'Sure can. I took her all the way up to Hell Roaring Rapids once. That's four hundred and eighty miles from the confluence of the Missouri.'

'Jeez.' Jack considered this. If he could take the steamer up to Fort Custer that would give him a 200-mile head start and he would be well out of the way of Horniblow. He could buy a new horse in Junction City on the north bank of the river opposite the Fort and head up to Bozeman and the mining towns of northern Montana. 'Hey, Cap, keep me a ticket. I'll be coming with ya.'

'We'll be pulling out at ten a.m.' Marsh hurriedly wandered off to find himself a chair, calling back, 'It's a fifty-dollar fare.'

'Sure, that's nothing to me.' Jack airily waved a hand. 'Or it *won't* be.' In his customary style, he hurled the bottle at the fire to childishly enjoy the explosion and make folks jump, and staggered drunkenly out. 'So long, all.'

In Poker Nell's there was a cosmopolitan array of punters around the tables: a Chinaman, Italian, Pole, Irishman, Mexican, a black former slave, now a cowboy. There was even a Sioux Indian, Red Bull, who was allowed in on condition he didn't imbibe. A professor of piano was rattling the ivories, and girls in skimpy costume were dancing with the customers and seeing to it they spent their cash liberally at the bar.

Behind the gaming-tables was a semicircle of raised boxes, curtained off with velvet drapes. These were worked by gals known as box-rustlers, who enticed randy punters inside, swishing the curtains

119

closed and obliging with forbidden caresses, often getting their sticky fingers on a wallet and passing it quickly through the curtain to an accomplice waiting outside. Only a week before a miner had had his throat slit in an argument about this.

'This is my kinda place,' Jack yelled out, spotting a busty wench known as Branded Kate, who, cigarette dangling from lips, was leaning on a chairback watching Nell deal a poker-game. Without ado, Scarface Jack gave a yell and picked Kate up to hoist her, kicking, over his shoulder. 'You ain't got *my* brand on ya yet, sister,' he shouted as he headed for the boxes. The players momentarily looked up, but Branded Kate's screams quickly ceased, so they carried on. Poker Nell frowned. That Jack Mosby again. And liquored up. Still, as long as he paid his dues, what the hell. . . .

Lonesome Bradshaw spent most of the morning with Rusty rounding up the scattered longhorns along the Powder River and settling them down as a herd again.

'What am I wasting my time for?' he muttered. 'I'd better go see what lawyer Horniblow's up to.'

'He won't be pleased when he hears what's been going on,' the red-haired cowboy opined. 'It's you who'll be under arrest, not me.'

'We'll see,' Brad said as they set off along the river for the ranch house. 'Maybe Horniblow will be in for a surprise.'

When they reached the Diamond Square late in the afternoon, however, it was Lonesome Bradshaw who was surprised to see Sheriff Biedler and the saloon-keeper, Rollins, standing by their horses talking to Horniblow. Rusty kneed his mount forward.

'I'm hell glad to see you, Sheriff,' he blurted out. 'There's been bad trouble. Danny Murphy and the boys are all dead. He's holding me prisoner.' He jerked his thumb back at Bradshaw. 'He shot 'em all down. Didn't give 'em a chance.'

'Maybe you'd better hear my side of the story,' Brad drawled, as he sat Blaze and leaned on the saddle horn. 'But, first, where are the wimmin?'

'The old un's gone to Miles City,' Horniblow replied. 'The young un's inside waitin' to say a tender goodbye to you.'

'Maybe you'd better come in,' Biedler said. 'Sounds like you been taking the law into your own hands again.'

Bradshaw stepped up on to the veranda and into the house. When she saw him the girl got up from her chair and rushed to him, hugging him.

'Oh, Brad, I've been worried about you. My aunt's sold out to Mr Horniblow. I didn't want to leave without explaining—'

'It's him who has the explaining to do,' the sheriff interrupted gruffly, 'about four innocent cowboys he's killed.'

Heather pulled herself away from him.

'That isn't true, surely?'

121

'Not exactly. Sure I killed 'em but only because they tried to kill me and were stealin' my cows.'

'What do you mean, *your* cows?' Horniblow asked. 'Sheriff, you had better 'cuff this man. He is a dangerous murderer and I want him off my property. When you get to Miles City make sure you swing him high.'

'Hold on.' Brad slipped his Remington out and held it, thumbing the hammer back, pointing the dangerous end at Biedler. 'Before you start the hanging, I'd like you all to clear off *my* property.'

'His property?' Horniblow laughed gruffly. 'What rubbish is he spinning now? This ranch is mine and I got the document here to prove it, signed, sealed and delivered. I paid one thousand dollars to Miss Monro's aunt only this morning.'

Brad gave his thin-lipped, crooked grin. 'Maybe it wasn't Aunt Maud's to sell. I'm sorry to have held back on you, Heather, but I needed to see the lie of the land. And it's pretty obvious now. This piece of offal, Horniblow, was behind the killing of your Uncle Rob.'

'What's he talking about now?' the lawyer protested.

'Quite simple. The ranch comes to me because I'm Rob's brother. That's the way he wanted it. I've got his will if you need any proof.'

Rollins had sidled behind Bradshaw in the crowded room and now he produced a nickle-plated two-shot derringer from his coat pocket and jabbed it into the Kansan's back.

'You better drop that six-gun, mister. This piece might be small but it can shatter your spine.'

'If I go, he goes,' Brad gritted out, keeping his Remington trained on Biedler.

Rusty stepped into the room behind Heather and put Brad's Spencer to her head. 'How about this bitch? Who's gonna save her?' He grinned wildly at the others. 'I got his guns from his hoss.'

Brad glanced at the girl through narrowed lids, then tossed the Remington revolver on to a sofa. 'It seems you win. Maybe we had better sort this out before the judge in town, Sheriff.'

'You ain't going nowhere,' Biedler replied, pulling out his iron handcuffs and forcing them over Bradshaw's wrists. 'Nor's she.'

'Whadda ya mean?' Brad muttered. 'You leave the girl outa this.'

'Oh, no, we're all in it together now.' Horniblow gave another caustic laugh. 'We're going to string you up, Bradshaw. You won't be getting no trial.'

'No need to tell me, you snake. You were behind all the rustling, getting these galoots to run off Rob's herd behind his back. Where'd you sell 'em? Down in Deadwood?'

'Why not?' Rusty grinned. 'Would you want to live on a cowpoke's wage? Mr Horniblow's taking us all into partnership. We'll have this spread and the Topaz once we've run off the greasers.'

'You made a poor job trying to kill Antonio del

Toro, and his son, and me for that matter. Maybe you ain't so clever. Who actually pulled the trigger, that's what I'd like to know?'

Rollins stepped out from behind him now that he was secure and beamed as he tugged at his moustache danglers. 'Who the hell you think? The Sheriff.'

'Yeah, I mighta guessed. That high-powered buffalo-gun.'

'You shut your mouth,' the big lawman exploded. 'You're too yappy for your own good, Sam.'

'Why worry, Sheriff.' Rusty gave a hoot of glee. 'We ain't gonna make a mistake this time. Where shall we hang him? From the barn rafter? After we've had our time with the gal, it'll be her turn.'

'I'm sorry, Heather. Looks like I've dug our graves. I shoulda warned you to go back to Boston. Now these rats have got the upper hand.' Brad sighed and shook his head. 'To tell the truth I couldn't really believe the marksman was Biedler, though I had my suspicions. Not the famous Sheriff "X". Not the man who cleared all of those badmen out of Virginia City, led the Montana vigilantes? How many was it you hanged? You've sure tarnished your reputation now, Sheriff. What'll folks say when they find out?'

'Shut up.' Biedler pushed him in the chest. 'Nobody's gonna find out. We'll bury you two out on the prairie. Look, I didn't really want in on this, but . . . what's a man to do? I'm gettin' old. What the hell use is a lawman's wage?'

124

'Tell me the old, old story,' Brad replied. 'Do I have to listen to your whines. You're just a murdering crook, that's all.'

Horniblow, Rusty and Sam Rollins looked very pleased with themselves and had relaxed now that the confrontation was over. Sheriff Biedler appeared a bit down in the mouth and had replaced his Colt revolver in its holster while he 'cuffed his prisoner. Suddenly, they all realized, the girl had moved in and whipped the gun. She was holding it double-handed, fumbling with the hammer, backing away from them, wavering it from one to the other.

'Run for it, Brad!'

Brad, from the corner of his eye, saw Rusty come up with his Spencer, aimed at the girl. He kicked out, sending it spinning from his hands. He swung his cuffed hands in a blow at Horniblow, knocking him aside. In a split second he realized there was no way he could get hold of the Colt from the girl before they all jumped on him. He would have to leave her. So he backed out of the door, locking it tight, before running for his horse.

He sent Blaze racing away, hanging on to the saddle as shots rang out from the farmhouse and whistled past his head. He jumped aboard and spurred the horse at a gallop back along the river bank the way he had come. He felt guilty about leaving Heather, but what else could he do?

They surely wouldn't risk raping and killing her. Not now with him on the loose. Surely it had been a bluff. No man in his right mind would do that to a girl like Heather. Not out here in the West. It was regarded as the most heinous of sins.

But was Horniblow in his right mind, or Biedler, or Rusty, or Rollins, for that matter? They were desperate men playing a desperate game.

Brad looked back over his shoulder as he galloped away. There was no sign of pursuit. Would they send Rusty after him? They must have had little trouble disarming Heather. Would they now try making their escape with the girl held as hostage? He could do little manacled and without his guns. He needed to get to Topaz ranch fast.

TEN

'Thank you.' Aunt Maud counted the ten crisp $100 greenbacks presented to her by the Wells Fargo teller, tucking them into her handbag. 'Now, perhaps, I can return to decent society.'

She emerged from the bank and took a look down Main Street, frowning at the state of it; deep mud, caused by recent rain and river flood, had been churned up by the chaotic traffic of covered wagons and bull-trains, by the frequenters of the saloons, stores, corral, livery, warehouses and dance-halls. So she took a right turn down Sixth Street, planning to cut around the back to reach the steamboat landing.

The street was better paved, but narrow and gloomy, and at each doorway there was a red light with some floozie in dishevelled, gauzy costume, padded bosom, painted face and little else lounging, cigarette in lips, watching her go by. There was something evil and dirty about the area and Maud was surprised to see a black-clothed preacher on a rickety box-podium, reading in a loud voice from his Bible.

Brother Van – as Methodist minister the Reverend William Wesley Van Orsdel was known – cried out to a bunch of giggling, half-dressed girls leaning out of a window above him.

'Beware, ye Jezebels, your name shall be covered with darkness. Come to me, repent now, or are you ready to suffer the torments of hell?'

'Why don't you come to us and taste a few torments yourself, preacher-man?' a slut with greasy face and hennaed hair taunted.

Maud stopped before him, prodding him with her parasol. 'Tell me, who are these impertinent creatures?'

'Madam?' Brother Van seemed surprised by the question. 'Best you do not enquire too closely. These are soiled doves.'

'Soiled doves?'

'Yes, fallen women. You have wandered into an area of sin and depravity. But they are not beyond redemption. The Lord has many mansions. At my mission I offer them refuge.'

'Who's the old haybag?' one of the doves cooed, amid screeches of hilarity. 'Your bedwarmer?'

Maud was shocked by the shower of profanities this initiated.

'How dare you speak to a man of God like that?' she shouted.

'Forgive them, sister, they know not what they say.' Brother Van rattled a wooden collecting-box at her.

'Can you help our cause in some small way? The costs of running the mission are steep. There are so many homeless unfortunates.'

'They've brought their misfortunes on themselves,' Maud snorted. 'They all look like they could do with a bath.'

However, she was suddenly touched by the good man's endeavours and produced a hundred-dollar bill, tucking it into the box. Her acidulous face broke into a smile as she waved goodbye.

'Good luck to you,' she called.

It was an odd feeling to be wealthy. Now, if she cut along this alleyway that surely would bring her to the river. She could hear the paddleboats close at hand blasting their steam sirens. Suddenly she heard running bootfalls from behind her. She turned and raised her parasol. A man loomed over her and she was struck violently on the side of her head. She stumbled against the wall; that was the last she knew as darkness closed over her.

Scarface Jack grinned his cracked teeth as he knelt and took the notes from her reticule. He gave a whistle and tucked them in his pocket – 900 smackers! He had followed her from the bank and whacked her with a sock filled with lead shot that he always carried in his coat pocket. Not a soul in sight. It was like taking candy from a baby. He jumped to his feet and hurried off to find *The Far West*.

The shallow-draught paddler was about to cast off as he ran up the gangplank and a black boy offered him a sack to wipe his muddy boots. Soon he was standing on the top deck watching Miles City disappear into a haze as they chugged on up the Yellowstone.

'Junction City, here we come.' He swaggered into the wheelhouse. 'Break out the brandy, Cap. I feel like a drink to celebrate.'

'It's no good,' Rusty shouted, panic in his voice, 'we've got to get out. He'll be back. He'll be bringing them dagos with him.'

'We can take them.' The big, bellicose Sheriff Biedler jutted out his jaw and, as they decided what to do, cleaned his long-barrelled rifle. 'I'll take first watch. I'll blast him out of the saddle first sight of him.'

'You don't know those greasers. They're crazy,' Rusty pleaded. 'They'll burn us down. And him . . . he's crazy, too. I'm going if you're not.'

Horniblow ground his teeth with frustration.

'Hot damn! He's right, X. The game's up for us here. We're never going to get our hands on this land now. We've got to cut our losses. We'll head across to the Yellowstone, follow it up to Bozeman, then on to Helena. There's plenty of rackets in that sweet city.'

'We've still got an ace,' Sam Rollins butted in, and pointed his cheroot at Heather. 'Her! He ain't gonna chance killin' her. She's our passport out.'

'Why don't you just go?' Heather shouted.

'Haven't you caused enough trouble? Haven't there been too many killings already? If you leave me he will be satisfied. I'm sure of it. But if you take me he'll come after you. He is not a man to give up. If you harm me, I pity you.'

Sheriff Biedler looked at the distraught girl.

'Right, let's go,' he said. 'But we're taking you with us. Get yourself a coat and be ready to ride, sister. Like Sam says, you're our ace in the pack.'

That had been the night before, when they were seated around, debating what to do. Now, Heather estimated, they were thirty miles or more away from the ranch and riding hard. The chance of any one catching up with them seemed minimal. Her body and legs ached from hanging on to the mustang, dragged along in their wake. Her first lesson in riding was proving painful. What next? They had reached the bank of a turbulent river, the Tongue she heard one say, and were plunging their mounts into it. Oh, no! she thought. How am I ever going to get across here? I will be swept away.

Swept from her saddle she was indeed by the torrent of icy water, but she hung on to the stirrup, gasping and kicking, and was dragged out on to the far bank like a drowning fish. Her long dress clinging to her, she was roughly bundled back on to the wet saddle by Biedler.

'Come on,' he roared. 'We ain't got time to stop and dry out.'

Then as they were crossing the smaller stream

called Moon Creek, they ran slap bang into Red Panther's band. The Indians came charging at them, whooping and wielding their tomahawks. Oh, God! Heather thought. It's out of the frying-pan into the fire!

'Are you all right?'

Maud returned from darkness to the modern world to look into the bearded face of Gary Gibbins, who was persistently shaking her shoulder.

'Am I all right? What do *you* think? Do I look as if I'm all right?' The old spinster put her hand to her throbbing head and felt something clammy.

'Blood! Help,' she croaked. 'I'm dying, that's what I am.'

'That's all right, sister.' The preacher man was kneeling beside Gibbins. 'You've had a nasty blow and a fall, but it's not serious.'

'Not serious? What do you mean, not serious? My time's up. Oh, please, will you give me a good head-stone? Oh, no!' Her bony fingers felt around for her bag. 'It's gone.' She started shrieking and crying. 'All my money.'

'Come, come, sister,' Brother Van chastized her. 'Money's not everything.'

'It might not be to you, but it is to me. Oh, my God!' she cried, realization dawning, sickeningly. 'I'm destitute. I have nothing. Whatever will happen to me?'

'Goldarn it, don't go on so.' Gary tried to soothe

132

her. 'If you ain't got no cash you can allus bed down in my place. I got a cosy li'l nook over the livery, if you don't object to a few bugs an' spiders' webs.'

'God forbid!' Maud cried, feeling as if she was about to swoon again.

It had been a long ride back to the Topaz. By the time Brad had had his handcuffs chiselled free, leaving just the wristbands, had explained what was going on, had found a new revolver and rifle, and had galloped back in the moonlight, Euala del Toro and her *vaqueros* alongside him ... the birds had flown.

'I'm going after them,' he shouted, transferring his saddle to the back of a stout pinto among stock in the corral – Blaze was tuckered out – 'they ain't got much of a head start.'

It was first light of dawn; the glowing east was promising a fair day. Euala jogged around on the magnificent Diablo, doing a figure of eight, changing his step, controlling him with a touch of her knees. An expert horsewoman she, too, looked magnificent, riding easy in the silver-bespangled saddle, her hands strong and yet gentle on the ornate bridle and bit. A martingale held down his arched neck and head, the balls of her small feet, in the handcrafted boots, rested in the leather *tapaderas* to protect her legs, the dangling fringes streaming in the wind. Today she wore a wide sombrero weighted with silver *conchos*, a white deerskin jacket and thin

cotton pants that clung to her shapely haunches and
legs. She flashed a gleaming smile at him as she
passed, showing off, proud of her skill and rightly so.

'She is beautiful eh?' Raoul kissed his clenched
fingers and offered her a salute. 'She is the only one
who can ride that horse. He killed a groom who
tried. His kick is like lightning. He is in love with her.
Who can blame him? She is too good for you,
gringo.'

Brad ignored him. Love and passion came in many
forms, that of the Spaniard different from the
American's. He had other things on his mind. The main
one being the safety of Heather. He slung the rifle over
his back and climbed on the pinto, patting his neck.

'C'mon, boy, we got a long ride ahead. Don't let
me down.'

'We are coming with you,' she cried, signalling to
her men to mount up.

'No.' He pulled the pinto round and faced them.
'This is my fight. I'm going it alone.'

The Mexican girl halted the snorting stallion and
frowned at him.

'We want to help.'

'No,' he growled. 'It ain't nuthin' to do with you.
It's up to me.'

'Let him go,' Raoul muttered. 'It is the gringo girl
he is interested in.'

Euala tossed her head, haughtily. 'They tried to
kill my father and brother. Kill them for me,
Americano.'

'I'll try.' Brad gave her a crooked grin. 'Wish me luck,' he called before setting the pinto off, leaping a fence and heading away along the river.

Euala watched him go.

'*Vaya con Dios*,' she whispered. She turned to Raoul, pointing a finger at him. 'You, keep out of my life. I am tired of you constantly watching me like a hawk.'

'It is the gringo girl he wants, cannot you see that, Euala? He is not interested in you.'

'Shut up,' she shouted, slashing her rawhide quirt at him. 'Don't you see? It is a matter of honour to him. He has to go.'

The band of white men had no chance to make a run, or use their rifles. As soon as Red Panther spotted them he put his cranesbill war flute to his mouth and gave a shrill whistle, leading the charge. Screaming for revenge the pack of twenty warriors hit them like a river in flood and from then on it was a mêlée of hand-to-hand fighting. Deaf Bull, as broad as a buffalo, crashed his pony into the young cowboy, Rusty, knocking him and his horse to the ground. He thrust his lance into him, watched him squirm, and jumped down. Red hair would make a fine trophy. He sliced the scalp and held it up, dripping blood, in triumph.

Sees-with-Ears was quick to tackle the saloon-keeper, Sam Rollins, but disappointed to see that he was as bald as an egg. Leaping on to him, knocking him from the saddle he held him down in the mud, his knife to his throat. But whites never fight fair. Rollins slipped a tiny pistol from his pocket and shot lead into Sees-With-Ears' guts. The brave would see no more with his ears or eyes.

The big Hairface with a tin star was a different matter, fighting bravely, using his heavy rifle as a club, swinging it about, fending off tomahawks and knives. He cracked Cold Hail's jaw and left him lying in the mud. He was a white man who knew how to fight. That was a fact. But the Indians had the weight of numbers and it was only a matter of time before they would drag him down like a pack of wolves around a bison.

The besuited lawyer, Horniblow, was causing most trouble with his revolver, choosing his target and firing with accuracy. He had already sent two of the younger braves to the other world. But it was only a matter of time before his gun was empty and then they would have him at their mercy.

Red Panther, for his part, after the initial fight, seemed more interested in the slender white girl. She had fallen from her horse and was backing away, her eyes staring with horror. She well knew what was in store for her. With a shrill yell of joy, Red Panther leapt upon her from his horse, dragging her down on to the grass. Here was a pretty piece to enjoy!

But why should he have her all to himself? Others of the warriors were distracted, going to watch as the white girl's dress was torn apart and she struggled beneath Red Panther. They urged him on, keen to be the next to have her after him . . . the redman and whiteman had certain priorities in common: whiskey and women! And, anyway the battle was almost won.

'Leave her!' Horniblow shouted at Sheriff Biedler. 'Make a run for it. Get out of here.'

Sheriff Biedler, fighting for his life against swinging tomahawks and flashing lances, glanced around. Yes, she would be a good diversion!

'Come on,' he roared, and swung on to his horse spurring him away.

Horniblow spent his last slug, sending a young warrior into eternity, his chest a gaping wound, and went racing away after him, charging across the prairie straight as an arrow.

The rain-damp ground had made it easy for Lonesome Bradshaw to follow the sign. At that moment he rode over the brow of low hills bordering Moon Creek. He had heard the screams and yells and already had the Mexican rifle in his hands, primed for use. Could that be Heather Monro down there? He saw the white gleam of her thigh above her stockings as a red-shirted Indian pinned her down and thrust her legs apart. Should he or shouldn't he? It was a dangerous shot. The slightest error and it could be the girl who died. Brad peered along the sights aligning the pinhead within the v-notch. A range of a good quarter of a mile.

Suddenly, as if to get a better position, or to bare himself, Red Panther raised himself up on his knees over Heather. Now! Brad had already taken half-pressure on the trigger and he squeezed it home without hesitation. The shot clapped out, the bullet whistled on its way, and Red Panther's head exploded like a canteloupe melon.

Almost simultaneously, as the Indians looked around and up at the shootist, there was the sound of a bugle and from around a bend in the creek a platoon of cavalry appeared, the US flag held proudly aloft as they charged, sabres drawn.

'Never fear,' Wraps-Up-His-Tail cried. 'They cannot hurt us. My magic will kill them. Watch!'

The startled Minneconjou stood their ground and watched, open-mouthed. The scrawny old medicineman, almost naked except for feathers and loincloth, stood erect pointing his sword at the oncoming 'Longknives'. But maybe it was a bad day for magic. Nothing happened. The cavalry didn't fall down. They just kept coming, the bugler going full blast. Sam Rollins ran towards them and one of the braves took the opportunity to put an arrow in his back. But the others didn't know what to do, some putting up a half show of aggression, others throwing away their weapons and raising their hands. The first to arrive were two Cheyenne scouts, lean young men in buckskins and decorations of their own. Wraps-Up-His-Tail waggled his sword at them: to his surprise to no avail. The Cheyenne sat their horses and laughed, then shot him down with their carbines.

Captain Hetherington held up his gauntleted

hand, yelling out a command to bring his cavalry platoon to a halt in circle around Heather as she tried to thrust away the almost headless body of Red Panther. Some of the hostiles had scattered for the hills, others were dead, the rest sullenly surrendering.

'Disarm them,' he shouted.

Lieutenant Claud Page leaped from his mount and ran to her, helping her unsteadily to her feet. Her face splattered with blood, her dress half-torn from her body, she held on to him.

'They didn't,' she gasped out. 'He didn't. I'm OK.' It seemed important to assure him that she was still a virgin.

'Thank God for that,' Page exclaimed, taking off his cavalry jacket to wrap around her. 'Miss Monro's all right,' he called to Hetherington. 'We got here in the nick of time, sir.'

'Not much of a fight for us, but never mind,' the captain replied, circling his horse around the body of the red-shirted warrior. 'So this is the infamous Red Panther. Not much to be afraid of now, is he?'

'Nah.' His sergeant guffawed. 'He was too interested in gettin' his end away. That was his downfall.'

'So, you're the marksman,' Hetherington said as Brad rode down from the bluff to join them. 'Very risky, but an excellent shot. No need to bother, though. We would have been here in time.'

'Glad you think so,' Bradshaw growled. He sat his horse and studied the girl who was shuddering from shock in Page's comforting arms. 'You'll be safe now, Heather.'

He swung the pinto around, nodding to his acquaintance, Kelly, who called:

'Where you going to?'

'After them two others,' Brad shouted, as he urged his horse away towards the Yellowstone.

ELEVEN

The boards of the *S.S. Far West* reverberated to the pounding of the engines as the churning rear paddle pushed them relentlessly up the flooded Yellowstone River. Scarface Jack stood in the bridgehouse with Captain Marsh at the wheel looking out at the wild country unfolding on either side.

'There's two hundred square miles of unbroken wilderness as far as the Musselshell,' the captain mused, waving his hand towards the north bank. 'There's game in profusion, sweetwater streams, and bitter alkali, too, pine-topped hills, and wide basins covered with brush and sage. When I first passed this way there were countless antelope feeding and the plains were black with buffalo.'

'Yeah, I seen it,' Jack remarked, but he was wondering what he would do with his new-found fortune. He could buy a saloon in Virginia City, have free whiskey and women for the rest of his life.

'We're seeing the last of the old West,' Grant

Marsh went on. 'Now the Sioux are subdued trade and industry is moving in. Cattlemen are taking over. Once the railroad arrives I'll be out of a job, too. These paddlers will be a thing of the past. The jerk-line teams as well. It will be all over.'

'Hey, Cap, there's a bunch of buffalo over there. It ain't over yet.'

'By God, there is.' A huge herd had appeared going at a fast trot along the southern riverbank. 'There's two riders coming through. That's why the beasts are moving. They must be hunters.'

Jack peered across at the horsemen who were cutting through the stragglers at the rear of the herd. One was a big, burly man in a macinaw, the other dressed more like a businessman.

'Chrissakes! They ain't hunters. It's that bastard Biedler and lawyer Horniblow.'

Jack went to the side of the boat and ducked down behind some bales. He watched the 'man-hunters' lope up and along the bank, waving frantically to the steamboat captain to heave to.

'Aye, it's the sheriff, sure enough,' Marsh said, catching the gleam of sunlight on the tin star Biedler sported on the front of his coat. 'It looks like they want us to pick 'em up.'

'Keep going,' Jack shouted back at him, drawing his six-gun, and waving it at the captain. 'Put on more steam. We ain't stopping to pick up nobody.'

He raised himself and aimed a shot at the two riders, wishing that he had thought to bring a carbine.

The bullet whanged close to them, kicking up mud, but doing little more than startle their horses.

'We ain't stopping for you dumb hicks,' Jack yelled, loosing off more lead and standing up to wave at them. 'So long, suckers.'

The captain, however, had other ideas, and began to turn the wheel, guiding the boat to the bank, calling down the speaking-tube to the engineer to cut the engines. He had had his doubts about Jack since he came aboard, the hints he had given about being in the money. He had been up to no good, that was for sure, and the sheriff was after him.

'What the hell you playing at?' Jack snarled as he returned to the wheelhouse. 'What are we slowing for? I told you to keep going for Junction City and fast.'

'I don't take orders from scum like you. You'd better put that pistol away. We'll see just what it is the sheriff wants.'

Jack smashed the revolver grip against the captain's bearded jaw, sending him sprawling.

'Don't try to be funny, smart-arse.' He grabbed the wheel and shouted down the speaking-tube. 'Is that the engine room? Put on speed, damn you.' He hung on to the wheel with one hand and pulled his knife from his belt with the other, pointing it at the captain. 'Get back here and do what I say. Or ye'll get this in your fat guts. You hear me?'

'This is piracy,' Grant Marsh muttered, feeling at his aching jaw and starting to get to his feet. 'You won't get away with it. I warn you, mister, get off this bridge, or else.'

'Shut up, dimwit,' Jack snarled. But he was horrified to see that the captain was coming up with a blunderbuss in his hands. He tried to hurl the knife but it was too late. The heavy naval gun exploded sending him through the bridge door to lie spread-eagled on the decking. Blood trickled from numerous small holes in his chest as he groaned, cursed and expired.

'Never thought I'd need to use it to quell a mutiny,' Captain Marsh bellowed when he had eased the *Far West* into the bank and the two men had brought their horses aboard. 'But I keep this ancient weapon handy in a cupboard just in case. What did you want him for?'

'Aw, the usual.' Sheriff Biedler knelt over Jack's corpse and frisked him, surprised to find the $800 in his pocket. Where had he got that from? 'Robbery,' he said, glancing along at Horniblow who had his back turned, unaware of what was going on. 'I'll return this to the rightful owner,' he muttered, and stuffed the wad into his pocket.

'Now, Captain, if you would be so good, we want to get to Junction City as fast as we can.'

'Very good, gents.' Grant moved the boat back out into the flood water, accepting one of the hundred-dollar bills generously offered by the sheriff for their fares. 'What you going to do with the stiffie? He's messing up my decking.'

144

'I'll feed him to the fishes.' Biedler laughed, hauling up Jack's corpse and toppling him over the rail into the water. 'He never was no good to nobody.'

'Well, I'll be jiggered,' Marsh exclaimed. 'There's another rider coming and it looks like he wants to come aboard too.'

'Don't stop. Keep on going. That's an order, Captain,' Biedler shouted. 'We ain't got time to stop for him.'

'Say, isn't it that fellow, what do they call him, Lonesome Bradshaw? What's he after.'

'He's another felon,' Sheriff Biedler replied. 'Just pile on steam. I'll deal with him.'

'A felon? What's he done?'

'Only murdered half a dozen men,' Horniblow snapped. 'He's a dangerous criminal. Keep going, Captain.'

Biedler was adjusting the sights on his rolling block Remington, a rifle with a 30-inch barrel and weighing eighteen pounds. He poked it over the boat's bulwarks and knelt down to squint through the telescope, waiting to get a good view of Bradshaw who was loping his pinto along the bank through clumps of diamond willow. His finger sensitive to the trigger, the sheriff had killed many a man, including Rob Henshall, from more than half a mile. But a moving target was a trickier business. Bradshaw kept moving in and out of the thicket, up and down the sloping bank.

'I'll let him get closer,' Biedler muttered.

145

Horniblow had pulled his revolver and crawled across the deck to join him.

'Make it a good shot, X. We need to see the end of this interfering fool.'

POW! The rifle boomed out, the .44-90-calibre slug whistling away across the water. It tore through the leaves of a willow, bringing a branch crashing down. Biedler waited, but Bradshaw came riding out of the other side.

'Damn!'

'For God's sake!' Horniblow was getting nervous, his palms sweating. The tall rider in the dark coat was like a pursuing avenger who would never give up. 'Can't you do better than that?'

Biedler licked his lips and fiddled with the rifle.

'Relax, I'll get him next time.'

But Bradshaw was not waiting to be shot from the saddle. He veered his horse away from the river, galloping hard, getting ahead of the paddler.

'He can't keep up that pace for long.'

He aimed the Long Tom again, crashing out a shot that kicked up dirt behind the horse's back heels, if anything urging it on faster. Biedler cursed loudly.

'What's he playing at?'

'You shoulda got him,' Horniblow moaned. 'We'll have to keep our eyes skinned round the next bend. He'll be waiting for us.'

'Just what is going on?' Captain Marsh shouted across at them as he stood at the wheel.

'Mind your own business,' Biedler yelled.

'It is my business. I don't want my ship being shot up.'

The sheriff ignored him, going to take a position for'ard near the prow of the boat.

'You keep back in the stern there, lawyer. Shoot to kill.'

'You don't need to tell me that,' Horniblow muttered unhappily, peering ahead at the angry, tossing waters.

Captain Marsh watched the broken trunk of a tree come floating along towards them. He pulled the wheel to starboard to try to avoid it. Not unusual at this time of the year; all sorts of debris was swept along in the murky yellow waters.

As the tree bumped along the *Far West*'s side Brad pulled himself up from the water and climbed on to the branches, his sodden clothes clinging to him. He made a wild leap and caught hold of an anchor chain. He hauled himself up and swung over the side.

'Howdy,' he said to Horniblow, who was kneeling with his back to him. The lawyer turned, startled, and Brad kicked the revolver from his hand before he could fire. He hauled him up and smashed in a piledriver to his jaw. The two hefty men traded punches as they had done once before, but this time it was a life-or-death struggle.

Sheriff Biedler turned from his vigil at the prow. He had seen the log but not Bradshaw lurking beneath it. Now to his surprise he saw him and

Horniblow struggling at the far end of the boat. He aimed the rifle at them. He didn't care which of them he killed. Suddenly, however, he felt a hard jab in his ribs. Captain Marsh had the business end of his blunderbuss stuck in his side.

'What are you doing, you fool?'

Grant Marsh looked along at the two men still swinging blows at each other. 'I told you not to shoot up my ship. You planning on blasting a hole in it? Anyway, that ain't fair, two against one. I'm warning you, Biedler, lay that gun aside.'

'You'll pay for this, Marsh,' the sheriff muttered, but laid the Remington down.

They watched as Bradshaw, his hair hanging over his eyes, connected with a wild southpaw to Horniblow's jaw. The lawyer staggered back. Brad hit him with a straight right and it was the end for Horniblow. The rail collapsed under his weight. He gave a scream as he went flying back and was caught in the churning paddles. He came back up again, his eyes aghast, his arms thrashing, and was swept away, bobbing on the surface and then disappearing below the waters.

'Looks like the river's taken him,' Marsh said. 'Now if you gentlemen got a quarrel why don't you have it out fair and square.'

Exhausted, blood trickling from his jaw, Brad tossed back his hair, and took a few tentative steps towards them. He peered at Biedler through his slits of eyes.

'How about it?' he growled.

The big sheriff hesitated, then a grin spread across his bearded face.

'Come on then.' He hauled his jacket back to reveal his holstered Colt. He knew there was a fifty-fifty chance Bradshaw's revolver was so damp it would misfire. He couldn't miss at forty paces. 'Let's go for it.'

Ker—ash! the sheriff's six-gun spurted flame and lead. But, a split second earlier Brad made a rolling dive along the deck, picked up Horniblow's revolver and came up shooting. Biedler fired again, but Brad was fanning the hammer to fast effect. Four accurately placed bullets in the heart sent the sheriff sprawling. He tried to raise his gun for one last shot, but collapsed back on the boards.

'That's the end of him,' Brad hissed, going to poke at his body with his foot. 'That's for Rob.'

'Who's Rob?'

'My brother. He killed him.'

'There's sure been a lot of killing. What shall we do with him. Give him to the river, too?'

'Yeah, why not.' Brad began to heft the sheriff up to a sitting position. 'He was a good man once, but he went bad.'

'Just a minute.' Grant Marsh felt in his jacket and produced his wallet. 'Eight hundred dollars in here that he took from Scarface Jack. It would be a shame to waste it.' He grinned at Brad. 'We could split it.'

'Nope, mister. I don't wan' it. Give it to Brother

149

Van for his orphanage.'

'I'll do that. What you gonna do, go back for your horse?'

'No, he can find his own way home.' A smile split Brad's face as he hurled the sheriff overboard and watched him wash away. 'All I want is dry clothes, a slice of smoked buffalo-tongue, and a bottle of brandy. Is that a deal?'

'That's a deal, mister. But first I better get back to the wheel. That boy, he ain't so hot as navigator. . . .'

TWELVE

The officers' mess at Fort Keogh was a scene of great gaiety, decorated with guidons and draperies, the post's military band playing martial airs, and a table groaning with a buffet supper beyond most settlers' dreams. The ladies were in new gowns imported from the East at considerable expense, the gentlemen wore ceremonial uniforms, sporting medals and gilt braid of rank.

On the bill of fare as starters were oysters, fried or raw, and vermicelli soup. There was a sumptuous display of roasts, turkey, beef, elk, mountain sheep or chicken-pie with platters of potatoes, and cranberry, lemon or plum sauce. Pastries came in the form of peach, strawberry, lemon or dried-apple pies topped with vanilla cream. And the guests, after sampling sherries, wines or the punch-bowl, could, if they could find space, finish with coffee, chocolate and jelly, fruit-cake or doughnuts.

'Pity there ain't no plum-duff,' Brad remarked to

151

Yellowstone Kelly. They were two of a number of civilians, ranchers, the Press, bankers and town commissioners, invited to the party.

The occasion was the visit to the fort of Lieutenant-General Philip Sheridan, commander of the military division of the Missouri, who was planning to visit the upper Yellowstone, with its geysers, or 'spitting fountains', which had recently been decreed the world's first national park.

He, a severe-looking man with a huge moustache, was remembered for the phrase: 'the only good Indian is a dead Indian'.

A martinet, who had encouraged the annihilation of the buffalo herds, he was in conversation nearby with General Nelson Miles, a hard fighter, but forgiving and kindly to his captives. In fact, Indian chiefs, in full regalia and war bonnets could often be seen wandering about the fort as they visited the log studio of the post photographer, Laton Huffman, who paid them for posing with tobacco.

'I think,' Sheridan said, 'we can congratulate ourselves that the Yellowstone basin has been pacified. What say you, Hetherington?'

'Yes, sir, now that Red Panther's dead. He was one of the worst of the hostiles,' the captain replied. 'But there are still isolated pockets of resistance and Sitting Bull's still skulking beyond the Canadian border.'

'Eternal vigilance,' Miles said. The party was also a farewell one for him. He was taking over the District of Columbia. 'That must be your watchword on the frontier.'

The dancing had begun and Brad caught sight of Heather Monro spinning around in the arms of Lieutenant Page. She certainly looked a picture in her low-cut dress of satin and lace. Kelly was reminiscing about their days up on the Shoshone River, exploring the Frozen Dog Hills.

'Why doncha come along as guide to the general?' he suggested.

'Nope, I'm too busy punchin' cows these days.'

When the music stopped Brad strode across to Heather. 'How about cutting a two-step with me if the loo-tenant don't object?' he drawled.

'I'm told you saved my life,' Heather remarked as they waltzed sedately around. 'I didn't know it at the time to thank you.'

'You look remarkably recovered.'

Heather flushed under his gaze.

'Why,' she asked, 'did your brother take the name of Henshall? That intrigues me.'

'Waal, he was one of the hated Kansan Redlegs during the war. There was no love lost 'tween them and the Missouri raiders. He pursued the William Quantrill gang when they sacked Lawrence and killed most of the male population. Jesse James was riding with them and he vowed to kill Rob. When a thug like Jesse makes a threat like that it ain't wise to take chances. Rob changed his name after the war and came north to start a new life.'

'Didn't Jesse threaten you?'

'No, I was just a kid in the war. I'm sorry about having to keep quiet about being his brother, only I had to find out what was going on. You know, Heather, there's no reason why we shouldn't still—'

'No, cousin. Ranching's not for me. Didn't you hear? Claud and I are engaged to be married. His father and Sheridan are old friends. The general's appointed Claud his aide-de-camp. So, soon we'll be living in Washington.'

'You don't say.' Brad led her back towards the punch bowl. 'This calls for a drink.'

'I'm not the one for you, Brad.' Heather squeezed his hand. 'You know who she is. Euala. You're two of a kind. The wild breed.'

'Euala del Toro?' Brad poured them drinks and shook his head. 'That crazy woman? You're joking.'

Gary Gibbins had spruced himself up in a striped suit bought from a catalogue, and had even taken a summer bath, a yearly event, and put on fresh long johns. He even went down on one knee when he proposed to Maud, who had been staying in his musty room, if not his bed.

'You may be a curmudgeonly ol' bat but I don't care,' he said romantically. 'I'm willin' to hitch my wagon to yourn.'

'That's very sweet of you. Don't think I'm not touched. It is the one regret of my life that I never wed. But no one ever asked and I turned against the breed.'

Maud's acidic features formed a puckered smile as she fluttered her lashes. 'Alas I must decline. I have decided to devote the rest of my life to joining Brother Van at his mission and trying to help those poor fallen women. I am teaching them needlework between the psalm-singing and finding honest work for them.'

'But Brother Van won't wed ye, woman. He ain't a marryin' man. Mind you, for a sam-singer he deals a straight pack. But a sam-singer he'll allus be.'

'You don't need me. You're an ornery old dyed-in-the-wool bachelor. But I've seen the light and I'm going to atone for my foolishness. Nonetheless,' Maud twitched her nose and leaned forward to kiss Gibbins' cheek, 'you've been very kind and I'm grateful.'

'Aw,' Gary muttered, taking out his teeth. 'I won't be needin' these in that case. They're fer eatin', not talkin'. But you ever change your mind I'll put 'em back in agin.'

Brad left the party early and in a hurry. It was a fine night. The Montana mists had been blown away and summer had arrived. He sent Blaze at a fast lope back across the prairie towards the Powder River, but when he reached the ranch he hardly paused. He changed horses and galloped on his way towards the Mizpah stream.

He raised a hand to the Mexican guard who challenged him.

'It's me. I'm a friend,' he shouted.

He galloped the horse up to the front of the house and shouted up at the darkened windows.

'Euala! Where are you?'

'What's going on?' Antonio del Toro poked out a rifle and craned his head from an open window.

'Howdy! I've had a great idea. Why don't you and me become partners, unite our holdings, form a cattle company, Antonio?'

'Are you drunk? Do you know what time it is? It's four in the morning.'

'No, I ain't drunk. I've come to see Euala. I got something to ask her.'

Euala suddenly unlocked the front door and stepped outside into the moonlight. She was in a white cotton nightdress, her black, shimmering hair hanging down her back almost to her waist.

'If you're not drunk you must be crazy,' she said.

'I am. Crazy in love. I been howlin' at the moon all the way over here.' He sat his horse, leaning on the saddle horn. 'I wancha to marry me.'

'Why, won't *she* have you?'

'It ain't that. Sure, I've seen her at the general's party. She's gonna marry that idjit Page. But she made me see who I really want. You.'

Euala considered this, pursing her lips as her father slammed his window shut. She strolled over to Brad and gave him a taunting smile.

'Why should *I* want you?'

'You know, this is the first time I seen you like this,

with your pants off.' He gave her a crooked grin, leaned down and scooped her up to sit on his knees. 'I like what I see.'

Euala linked her arms around his neck and kissed him as he turned the horse and rode away.

'It will be dawn by the time we reach the Diamond Square,' she whispered. 'Do you want breakfast first, or. . . ?'

He kissed her hair and her neck, gripping her tight as the horse cantered away along the stream.

'The "or" sounds good,' he said.

ABERDEEN
CITY
ARIES